The Mysteries of

GW01326417

A Novel of In

Volume 1

T. W. Speight

Alpha Editions

This edition published in 2024

ISBN : 9789361479298

Design and Setting By
Alpha Editions
www.alphaedis.com
Email - info@alphaedis.com

As per information held with us this book is in Public Domain.
This book is a reproduction of an important historical work. Alpha Editions uses the
best technology to reproduce historical work in the same manner it was first
published to preserve its original nature. Any marks or number seen are left
intentionally to preserve its true form.

Contents

CHAPTER I.

GILBERT DENISON'S WILL

The First Gentleman in Europe sat upon the throne of his fathers, and the Battle of Waterloo was a stupendous event that still dwelt freshly in men's memories, when one bright August evening, Gilbert Denison, gentleman, of Heron Dyke, Norfolk, lay dying in his lodgings in Bloomsbury Square, London.

He was a man of sixty, and, but a few days before he had been full of life, health, and energy. As he was riding into town from Enfield, where he had been visiting some friends, his horse slipped, fell, and rolled heavily over its rider. All had been done for Gilbert Denison that surgical skill could do, but to no avail. His hours were numbered, and none knew that sad fact better than the dying man. But in that strong, rugged, resolute face could not be read any dread of the approaching end. He was a Denison, and no Denison had ever been known to fear anything.

By the bedside sat his favourite nephew and heir, whose christian name was also Gilbert. He was a young man of three or four and twenty, with a face which, allowing for the difference in their years, was, both in character and features, singularly like that of his uncle. Gilbert the younger was not, and never had been, a handsome man; but his face was instinct with power: it expressed strength of will, and a sort of high, resolute defiance of Fortune in whatever guise she might present herself. This young man carried a riding-whip in his hand; on a table near lay a pair of buckskin gloves. He wore Hessian boots with tassels, and a bottle-green riding-coat much braided and befrogged. His vest was of striped nankin, and he carried two watches with a huge bunch of seals pendant from each of them; while over the velvet collar of his coat fell his long hair. His throat was swathed in voluminous folds of soft white muslin, tied in a huge bow, and fastened with a small brooch of brilliants. Our young gentleman evidently believed himself to be a diamond of the first water.

The August sun shone warmly into the room; through the half-open windows came the hum of traffic in the streets; a vagrant breeze, playing at hide-and-seek among the heavy hangings of the bed, brought with it a faint odour of mignonette from the boxes on the broad window-sills outside. A hand of the dying man sought a hand of his nephew, found it, and clasped it. The latter had been expressing his sorrow at finding his uncle in so sad a state, and his hopes that he would yet get over the results of his accident.

"There is no hope of that, boy," said Mr. Denison. "A few hours more, and all will be ended. But why should you be sorry? Is the heir ever really sorry when he sees the riches and power, which all his life he has been taught will one day be his, coming at last into his own grasp? Human nature's pretty much the same all the world over."

"But I am indeed heartily sorry; believe me or not, uncle, as you like."

"I will try to believe you, boy," said Mr. Denison with a faint smile, "and that, perhaps, will answer the same purpose."

There was silence for a little while, then the sick man resumed.

"Nephew, this is a sad, wild, reckless life that you have been leading in London these four years past."

"It is all that, uncle."

"Had I lived, what would the end of it have been?"

"Upon my word I don't know. Utter beggary I suppose."

"How much money are you possessed of?"

"I won a hundred guineas the other night at faro. I am not aware that I possess much beyond that."

"And your debts?"

The young man mused a moment.

"Really, I hardly know to a hundred or two. A thousand pounds would probably cover them, but I am not sure."

"A thousand pounds! And I have paid your debts twice over within the last four years!"

Gilbert the younger smiled.

"You see, uncle, the schedule I sent you each time was not a complete one. I did not care to let you know every liability."

"You did not expect me to assist you again?"

"Certainly not, sir, after the last letter you wrote to me. I knew that when you wrote in that strain you meant what you said. I should never have troubled you again."

"After your hundred guineas had gone--and they would last you but a very short time--what did you intend to do?"

"I had hardly thought seriously about it. Perhaps the fickle goddess might have smiled on me again. If not, I should have done something or other. Probably enlisted."

"Enlisted as a common soldier?"

"As a common soldier. I don't know that I'm good for much else."

"But all that is changed now. Or at least you suppose so."

"I suppose nothing of the kind, sir," said the young man, hotly.

"As the master of Heron Dyke, with an income of six thousand a year, you will be a very different personage from a needy young rake, haunting low gaming-tables, and trying to pick up a few guineas at faro from bigger simpletons than yourself."

Gilbert the younger sprang to his feet, his lips white and quivering with passion.

"Sir, you insult me," he said, "and with your permission I will retire."

And he took up his hat and gloves.

"Sit down, sir--sit down, I say," cried the elder man, sternly. "Don't imagine that I have done with you yet."

"I have never been a frequenter of low gaming-houses; I have never cheated at cards in my life," said the young man, proudly.

"You would not have been a Denison if you had cheated at cards. But again I tell you to sit down. I have much to say to you."

Gilbert the younger did as he was told, but with something of an ill grace. In his eyes there was a cold, hard look that had not been there before.

"Nephew, if you have not yet disgraced yourself--and I don't believe that you have--you are on the high-road to do so. Has it ever entered your head to think whither such mad doings as yours must inevitably land you?"

"I suppose that other men before me have sown their wild oats," said Gilbert, sulkily. "I have heard it said that you yourself, sir----"

"Never mind me. The question we have now to consider is that of your future. When you are master of Heron Dyke--if you ever do become its master--is it your intention to make ducks and drakes of the old property, as you have made ducks and drakes of the fortune left you by your father?"

"Really, sir, that is a question that has never entered into my thoughts."

"Then it is high time that it did enter them. I said just now 'If you ever do become the master of Heron Dyke.'"

"Is that intended as a threat, sir?" asked Gilbert, a little fiercely.

"Never mind what it is intended as, but listen to me. I presume you are quite aware that it is in my power to leave Heron Dyke to anyone whom I may choose to nominate as my heir--to the greatest stranger in England if I like to do so?"

"I am of course aware that the property is not entailed," said the other, stiffly.

"And never has been entailed," said Mr. Denison with emphasis. "It has come down from heir male to heir male, for six hundred years. Providence having blessed me with no children of my own, by the unwritten law of the family the property would descend in due sequence to you. But that unwritten law is one which I have full power to abrogate if I think well to do so. Such being the case, ask yourself this question, Gilbert Denison: 'Judging from my past life for the last four years, am I a fit and proper person to become the representative of one of the oldest families in Norfolk? And would my uncle, taking into account all that he knows of me, be really justified in putting me into that position?'"

The elder man paused, the younger one hung his head.

"I think, sir, that the best thing you can do will be to let me go headlong to ruin after my own fashion," was all that he said.

"You will be good enough to remember that I have another nephew," resumed the dying man. "There is another Gilbert Denison as well as yourself."

"Aye! I'm not likely to forget him," said the other, savagely.

"So! You have met, have you? Well, from all I have heard of my brother Henry's son, he is a clever, industrious, and well-conducted young man--one not given, as some people are, to wine-bibbing and all kinds of riotous living. Had you been killed in a brawl, which seems a by no means unlikely end for you to come to, he would have stood as the next heir to Heron Dyke."

Young Gilbert writhed uneasily in his chair; the frown on his face grew darker as he listened.

"And even as matters are," resumed his uncle, blandly, "even though you have not yet come to an untimely end, it is quite competent for me to pass you over and nominate your cousin as my heir."

"Oh, sir, this is intolerable!" cried the young man, starting to his feet for the second time. "To see you as you are, uncle, grieves me to the bottom of my heart--believe me or not. But I did not come here to be preached at. No man knows my faults and follies so well as I know them myself. Leave your property as you may think well to do so; but I hope and pray, sir, that you will never mention the subject to me again."

He turned to quit the room, and had reached the door, when he heard his uncle's voice call his name faintly. Looking back, he was startled to see the change which a few seconds had wrought in the dying man. His eyes were glassy, the pallor of his face had deepened to a deathlike whiteness. Gilbert was seriously frightened: he thought the end had come. There was some brandy in a decanter on the little table. It was the work of a moment to pour some into a glass. Then, with the aid of a teaspoon, he inserted a small portion of the spirit between the teeth of the unconscious man. This he did again and again, and in a little while he was gratified by seeing some signs of returning life. There was an Indian feather-fan on the chimney-piece. With this, having first flung the window wide open, he proceeded to fan his uncle's face. Presently Mr. Denison sighed deeply, and the light of consciousness flickered slowly back into his eyes. He stared at his nephew for a moment as though wondering whom he might be, smiled faintly, and pointed to a chair.

Gilbert took one of his uncle's clammy hands in his, chafed it gently for a little while, and then pressed it to his lips. "You are better now, sir," he said.

"Yes, I am better. 'Twas nothing but a little faintness. I shall not die before tomorrow night." He lay for a little while in silence, gazing up at the ceiling like one in deep thought. Then he said, "And now about the property, Berty."

The young man thrilled at the word. His uncle had not called him by that name since he was quite a lad. "Oh, sir, do not trouble yourself any more about the property," he cried. "Whatever you have done, you have no doubt done for the best."

"But I want to tell you what I have done, and why I have done it. To-morrow I may not have strength to do so." Young Gilbert moved uneasily in his chair. The sick man noticed it. "Impatient of control as ever," he said, with a smile. "Headstrong--wilful--obstinate; you are a true Denison. Measure me a dose out of that bottle on the chimney-piece. It will give me strength."

Gilbert did as he was bidden, and then resumed his seat by the bedside.

"It was not a likely thing, my boy, that I should leave the estate away from you," resumed Mr. Denison; and, despite all his self-control, a sudden light leapt into Gilbert's eyes as he heard the words. "Notwithstanding all your wild ways and outrageous carryings on, I have never ceased to love you. You have been to me as my own son; as your father was to me a true brother. As for Henry, although he is dead, there was no love lost between us. We quarrelled and parted in anger, as we should quarrel and part in anger again were he still alive. I do not want to think that a son of his will ever call Heron Dyke his home."

Young Gilbert's face darkened again at the mention of his cousin's name. As between the two brothers years ago there had been a feud that nothing had ever healed, so between the two cousins there had arisen a deadly enmity which nothing in this world (so young Gilbert vowed a thousand times to himself) should ever bridge over. They were good haters, those Denisons, and never more so than when they had quarrelled with one of their own kith and kin.

"No, the old roof-tree shall be yours, Gilbert, and all that pertains to it," continued Mr. Denison, "as you will find when my will comes to be read. You will find, too, a good balance to your credit at the bank, for I have not been an improvident man. At the same time I have had expenses and losses of which you know nothing. But--there is a 'but' to everything in this world, you know--you will find in my will a certain proviso which I doubt not you will think a strange one, most probably a hard one, and which I feel sure you will at first resent almost as if I had done you a personal injury. It has not been without much thought and deliberation that the proviso I speak of has been embodied in the will, but I fully believe that twenty years hence, should you live as long, you will bless my memory for having so introduced it."

Mr. Denison lay back for a moment or two to gather breath. His nephew spake no word, but sat with his eyes bent studiously on the floor.

"Gilbert, as a rule we Denisons are a long-lived race," resumed the dying man, "and but for this unhappy accident, I have a fancy that I should have worn for another score years at the least. If you have ever been at the trouble to read the inscriptions on the tombs of your ancestors in Nullington Church, you must have noticed how many of them lived to be seventy-five, eighty, and in some cases ninety years of age. Now, what prospect or likelihood is there of your living to be even seventy years old? Your constitution is impaired already. That dark, sunken look about the eyes, those fine-drawn lines around the mouth, what business have they there at your age? I tell you, Gilbert Denison, that if you do not change your mode of life at once and for ever, you will not live to see your thirtieth birthday. And what probability is there that you will change it? That is the question that I have asked myself, not once, but a thousand times. If this wild and reckless mode of life has such fascinations for you, that it has induced you to dissipate the fortune left you by your father, to apply to me more than once to extricate you from your difficulties, to involve you deeply with the money-lenders, and to bring you at length to contemplate I know not what as a mode of escape from your troubles, what sort of hold will it have over you when you come into the uncontrolled possession of six thousand a year? That is a problem which I, for my part, cannot answer."

Mr. Denison paused as though he expected a reply to his last question. There was silence for a little while, and then the nephew spoke in a low, constrained voice.

"I can only repeat, sir, what I said before: that you had better let me go headlong to ruin my own way."

"Not so. I have told you already that I have made you my heir. Heron Dyke, and all that pertains to it, will call you master in a few short hours. It----" but here he broke off for a moment to overcome some inward emotion. "I shall never see the old place again, and I had such schemes for the next dozen years! Well--well! we Denisons are not children that we should cry because our hopes are taken from us."

"Sir, is not this excitement too much for you?" asked the nephew.

But the other cleared his voice, and went on more firmly than before:

"Yes, Gilbert, the old roof-tree and the broad acres shall all be yours, and long may you live to enjoy them. That is now the dearest wish left me on earth."

"But the proviso, sir, of which you spoke just now?" said the young man, whose curiosity was all aflame.

"The proviso is this: That should you not live to be seventy years of age, the estate, and all pertaining to it, shall pass away from you and yours at your death, and go to your cousin, the son of my brother Henry; or to his heirs, should he not be alive at the time. But should you overpass your seventieth birthday, though it be but by twelve short hours, the estate will remain yours, to will away to whom you please, or to dispose of as you may think best."

Gilbert Denison stared into his uncle's face, with eyes which plainly said: "Are you crazy, or are you not?"

"No, Gilbert, I am not mad, however much, at this first moment, you may be inclined to think me so," said Mr. Denison with a faint smile, as he laid his fingers caressingly on the young man's arm. "I told you before, that I had not done this thing without due thought and deliberation. It is the only mode I can think of to save you from yourself, to tear you away from this terrible life of dissipation, and to make a man of you, such as I and your father, were he now alive, would like you to become. I have given you something to live for; I have put before you the strongest inducement I can think of to reform your ways. Once on a time you had a splendid constitution, and seventy is not a great age for a Denison to reach. In due time you will probably marry and have a son. That son may be left little better off than a pauper should his father not live to see his seventieth birthday. If I cannot induce you to take care of your health for your own sake, I will try to induce you to do so for the sake of those who will come after you. Heaven only knows whether my plan will succeed. Our poor purblind schemes are but feeble makeshifts at the best."

"In case I should fall in the hunting-field, sir, or----"

"Or come to such an untimely end as I have come to, eh? Should you meet with your death by accident, and not by your own hand, the special stipulation in the will which I have just explained to you will become invalid, and of no effect. You will find this and other points duly provided for. Nothing has been forgotten."

There ensued a silence. The sick man suddenly broke it.

"Perhaps some scheme may enter your head, Gilbert, of trying to upset the will after I am dead? But you will find that a difficult matter to do."

"Now, Heaven forbid, sir," cried the young man, vehemently, "that such a thought should find harbourage in my brain for a single moment! You think me worse than I am. You do not know me: you have never understood me."

"Do we ever really understand one another in this world? We are so far removed from Heaven, that the lights burn dimly, and we see each other but as shadows walking in the dusk."

At this moment there was a ring below stairs, then a knock at the chamber door, and in came the nurse. The doctor was waiting.

"You had better go now, my boy," said Mr. Denison, pressing Gilbert's hand affectionately. "At ten tomorrow I shall expect to see you again."

Gilbert Denison stood up and took the dying man's fingers within his strong grasp; he gazed with grave, resolute eyes into the dying man's face.

"One moment, sir. As I said before--you do not know me. You have seen one side of me--the weak side--and that is all. If you think that, when I make up my mind to do so, I cannot throw off the trammels of my present life, almost as easily as I cast aside an old coat, then, sir, you are quite and entirely mistaken. That I have been weak and foolish I fully admit, but it is just possible, sir, that, young as I am, I may have had trials and temptations of which you know nothing. How many men before me have striven to find in reckless dissipation a Lethe for their troubles? Not that I wish to excuse myself: far from it. I only wish you to understand and believe, uncle, that there is a side to my character of which as yet you know nothing."

"I am willing to believe it, Gilbert," was the answering murmur: and once more the young man pressed Mr. Denison's hand to his lips.

When Gilbert Denison called in Bloomsbury Square the following morning he found his uncle much weaker and more exhausted. Mr. Denison was evidently sinking fast. Gilbert stayed with him till the end. A little while before that end came, he drew his nephew down to him and spoke in a whisper:

"Never forget the motto of your family, my boy: 'What I have, I hold.'"

And before the sun rose again, Gilbert Denison the younger was master of Heron Dyke, with an income of six thousand a year.

CHAPTER II.

MRS. CARLYON AT HOME

Forty-five years, with all their manifold changes, had come and gone since Squire Denison, of Heron Dyke, died in his lodgings in Bloomsbury Square, London.

It was the height of the London season, and at Mrs. Carlyon's house at Bayswater a small party were assembled in honour of the twenty-first birthday of her niece, Miss Ella Winter. Mrs. Carlyon, who had been a widow for several years, was still a handsome woman, although she could count considerably more than forty summers. Her house was a good one, pleasantly situated, and well furnished. She kept her brougham and half-a-dozen servants, and nothing pleased her better than to see herself surrounded by young people. Most enjoyable to her were those times when Miss Winter was allowed by her great-uncle, the present Squire Denison, of Heron Dyke, to exchange for a few weeks the quietude of the country for the gaieties of Bayswater and the delights of the London season. Such visits, however, were few and far between, and were appreciated accordingly.

To-day some ten or a dozen friends were dining with Mrs. Carlyon. One of them was little Freddy Bootle, with his little fluffy moustache, his eye-glass, and his short-cut flaxen hair parted down the middle. Freddy was universally acknowledged to be one of the best-hearted fellows in the world, and one of the most easily imposed upon. He was well connected, and was a junior partner in the great East-end brewery firm of Fownes, Bootle and Bootle. He was in love with Miss Winter, and had proposed to her a year ago. Although unsuccessful in his suit, his feelings remained unchanged, and he was not without hope that Ella would one day look on him with more favourable eyes. Ella and he remained the best of friends. That little episode of the declaration in the conservatory, which to him had been so momentous an affair, had been to her no more than a passing vexation.

Another of the gentlemen whom it may be as well to introduce is Philip Cleeve, son of Lady Cleeve, of Homedale, near Nullington. He and Miss Winter are great friends. Philip is in love with Maria Kettle, the only daughter of the Vicar of Nullington. What a handsome fellow he is, with his brown curling hair, his laughing hazel eyes, and his ever-ready smile. Ella sometimes wonders how Maria Kettle can resist his pleasant manners and fascinating ways. There is no more general favourite anywhere than Philip Cleeve. The worst his friends could say of him was that he was given to be a little careless in money matters--and his purse was a very slender one. Between ourselves,

Philip was sometimes hard up for pocket-money: though, perhaps, these same friends suspected it not.

Dinner was over, and the ladies had returned to the drawing-room, when Mrs. Carlyon was called downstairs, and a couple of minutes later Ella was sent for. A gentleman had called, Captain Lennox, bringing with him a birthday gift for Ella, from Mr. Denison, of Heron Dyke. The Captain had accidentally met Mr. Denison the day previously, and happening to mention that he was about to run up to London on a flying visit, the latter had asked him to take charge of and deliver to his niece a certain little parcel which he did not feel quite easy about entrusting to the post. This parcel the Captain now delivered into Ella's hands. On being opened, the contents proved to be a pair of diamond and pearl ear-rings.

Mrs. Carlyon at once gave Captain Lennox a cordial invitation to join the party upstairs, which he as cordially accepted. They had never met before; but Ella had some acquaintance with the Captain and his widowed sister, who lived with him in Norfolk. The Captain and his sister had come strangers to Nullington some six months previously, and finding the place to their liking, had, after a fortnight's sojourn at an hotel, taken The Lilacs, a pretty cottage ornée. Captain Lennox was a tall, thin, fair-haired man about forty years of age. He had clear-cut aquiline features, wore a moustache and long whiskers, and was always faultlessly dressed.

"How was my uncle looking, Captain Lennox?" asked Ella, somewhat anxiously, when the ear-rings had been duly examined and admired.

"Certainly quite as well as I ever saw him look."

"I am glad of that. I had a letter from him three days ago, in which he said that he had not felt better for years. But that is a phrase he nearly always makes use of when he writes to me. He does it to satisfy me. When his health is in question, Uncle Gilbert's statements are sometimes to be taken with a grain of salt."

"Now that Captain Lennox has assured you that your uncle is no worse than usual, you can afford to give me another week at Bayswater," said Mrs. Carlyon.

Ella smiled and shook her head.

"I must go back next Monday without fail."

"You are as obstinate as the Squire himself," cried her aunt. "I have a great mind to write and tell him that he need not expect you before the twentieth."

"He will expect me back on the thirteenth," said Ella. "And I would not disappoint him for a great deal."

"Well, well, you must have your own way, I suppose. All the same, it is a great deprivation to me. But those good people upstairs will think that I am lost, so come along, both of you."

At this juncture a fresh arrival was announced. It was Mr. Conroy, special artist and correspondent for *The Illustrated Globe*, whose vivid letters from the seat of war had been so widely read of late. Mrs. Carlyon received him with warmth.

"I hope you have brought some of your sketches with you, as you so kindly promised," she said, when greetings were over.

"My portfolio is in the hall," he replied. "But you must not expect to see anything very finished. In fact, my sketches are all in the rough, just as I jotted them down immediately after the events I have attempted to portray."

"That will only serve to render them the more interesting. They will seem like veritable pulsations of that awful struggle," said Mrs. Carlyon, as she rang the bell and ordered the portfolio to be brought upstairs. Then she introduced Conroy to her niece, Miss Winter: and he gave a perceptible start.

"They have met before," thought Captain Lennox to himself. He was looking on from his seat close by, and he watched narrowly for a gleam of recognition between them. But no such look came into the eyes of either. The Captain, who had a keen nose for anything not above board, turned the matter over in his mind. "That start had a meaning in it," he mused. "There's more under the surface than shows itself at present."

Conroy never forgot the picture that stamped itself on his memory the first moment he set eyes on Ella Winter. He saw before him a tall, slender girl, whose gait and movements were as free and stately as those of a queen. She had hair of the colour of chestnuts when at their ripest, and large luminous eyes of darkest blue. The eyebrows were thick and nearly straight, and darker in colour than her hair. Her face was a delightful one in the mingled expression of gravity and sweetness--the gravity was often near akin to melancholy--that habitually rested upon it. A forehead broad, but not very high; a straight, clear-cut nose with delicate nostrils; lips that were, perhaps, a trifle over-full, but that lacked nothing of purpose or decision; a firm, rounded chin with one dainty dimple in it: such was Ella Winter as first seen by Edward Conroy. This evening she wore a dress of rich but sober-tinted marone, relieved with lace of a creamy white.

"I have often wished to see her," muttered Conroy to himself. "Now I have seen her, and I am satisfied."

Mrs. Carlyon had the portfolio taken into her boudoir so as to be clear of the music and conversation in the larger room, and there a little group gathered round to examine and comment upon the sketches, and to listen to Conroy's few direct words of explanation whenever any such were needed.

Ella stood and looked on, listening to Mr. Conroy's remarks and to the comments of those around her, and only giving utterance to a monosyllable now and then. "This man differs, somehow, from other men," was her unspoken thought. "He is a man carved out by hand; not one of a thousand turned out by lathe, and all so much alike that you cannot tell one from another. He has individuality. He interests me."

She was taking but little apparent interest in what was going on before her; but, for all that, she lost no word that was said. She stood, fan in hand, her arms crossed before her, her fingers interknit, her eyes, with a look of grave, sweet inquiry in them, bent on Conroy's face. "Aunt shall ask him to leave his portfolio till tomorrow," she thought, "and after these people are gone I can have his sketches all to myself."

Conroy was indeed of a different mould from those butterflies of fashion who ordinarily fluttered around Miss Winter. He was certainly not a handsome man, in the general acceptation of the term. His face was dark and somewhat rugged for a man still young, but lined with thought, and instinct with energy. He had seen his twenty-eighth birthday, but looked older. Edward Conroy had gone through much hardship and many dangers in the pursuit of his profession. Already his black hair was growing thin about the temples, and was streaked here and there with a fine line of grey. The predominant expression of his face was determination. He looked like a man not easily moved--whom, indeed, it would be almost impossible to move when once he had made up his mind to a certain course. And yet his face was one that women and children seemed to trust intuitively. At times a wonderful softness, an expression of almost feminine tenderness, would steal into his dark brown eyes. Tears had nothing to do with it: he was a man to whom tears were unknown. The sweetest springs are those which lie farthest from the surface and are the most difficult to reach. From the first, Ella felt that she had to contend against a will that was stronger than her own, From the first she could not help looking up to and deferring to Edward Conroy, as she had never deferred to any man but her uncle. Probably she liked him none the less for that.

When Conroy's sketches had been looked at and commented upon, the majority of the company went back into the drawing-room. Dancing now began, and Ella found herself engaged to one partner after another. Conroy sat down in a corner of the boudoir next to old-fashioned, plain-looking Miss Wallace, whom nobody seemed to notice much, and was soon deep in conversation with her. Ella was annoyed two or three times at detecting herself looking round the room and wondering what had become of him.

Somehow she seemed to pay less attention than usual to the small-talk of her partners. They found her indifferent and distrait.

"She may be rich, and she may be handsome," remarked young Pawson of the Guards to one of his friends, "but she is not the kind of woman that I should care to marry. She has a way of freezing a fellow and making him feel small; and that's uncomfortable, to say the least of it."

By-and-by Conroy strolled into the drawing-room, and Captain Lennox, who happened to be watching Ella at the time, saw the sudden light that leapt into her eyes the moment she caught sight of his form in the doorway.

"She's interested in him already," muttered the Captain to himself. "This Mr. Conroy is playing some deep game, or I am very much mistaken. I wonder where he has met her before?"

"How do you think my niece is looking?" asked Mrs. Carlyon of Captain Lennox, a little later on, as she glanced fondly at Ella.

"Uncommonly well," replied the Captain. "She always does look well."

"Ah no, not always. She was not looking well when she came to me."

Captain Lennox considered. He also glanced across at Ella.

"I have noticed one thing, Mrs. Carlyon--that she has at times a strangely grave look in her eyes for one so young. It is as if she had something or other in her thoughts that she finds difficult to forget."

"That is just where the matter lies. How *can* she forget? Since that strange affair that happened last February at Heron Dyke----"

"Oh, that was a regular mystery," interrupted the Captain, aroused to eager interest. "It is one still."

"And it has left its effects upon poor Ella. A mystery: yes, you are right in calling it so; sure never was a greater mystery enacted in melodrama. Ella's stay with me has, no doubt, benefited her in a degree, but I am sure it lies in her thoughts almost night and day."

"Well, it was a most unaccountable thing. I fancy it troubles Mr. Denison."

"It must trouble all who inhabit Heron Dyke. For myself, I do not think I could bear to live there. Were it my home I should leave it."

Captain Lennox stroked his fair whiskers in surprise.

"Leave it!" he exclaimed. "Leave Heron Dyke!"

"*I* should. I should be afraid to stay. But then I am a woman, and women are apt to be timorous. If--if Katherine----"

Mrs. Carlyon broke off with a shiver. She rose from her seat and moved away, as though the subject were getting too much for her.

A strange mystery it indeed was, as the reader will admit when he shall hear its particulars later. But it was not the greatest mystery enacted, or to be enacted, at Heron Dyke.

"I have a favour to ask you, Mr. Conroy," began Ella, when they found themselves apart from the rest for a moment.

"You have but to name it," he answered, a smile in his speaking eyes as they glanced into hers.

"Will you let your portfolio remain here until tomorrow? I want to look at the sketches all by myself."

"They interest you?"

"Very much indeed. How I should like to have been in Paris during that terrible siege!"

"You ought to be thankful that you were a hundred miles away from it."

"But surely I might have been of some sort of use. I could have nursed among the wounded--or helped to distribute food to the starving--or read to the dying. I should have found something to do, and have done it."

"Still, I cannot help saying that you were much better away. You can form but a faint idea of the terror and agony of that awful time."

"But there were women who went through it all, and why should not I have done the same? My life seems so useless--so purposeless. I feel as if I had been sent into a world where there was nothing left for me to do."

"So long as poverty and sickness, want and misery abound, there is surely enough to do for earnest workers of every kind."

"But how to set about doing it? I feel as if my hands were tied, and as if I could not cut the cord that binds me."

"And yet your life is not without its interests. Your uncle, for instance----"

"You have heard about my uncle!" she said, in her quick way, looking at him with a little surprise.

"Yes, I have heard of Mr. Denison, of Heron Dyke. There is nothing very strange in that."

"Ah, yes, I think I am of some use to him," said Ella, softly. "I could not leave Uncle Gilbert for anything or anybody. And I have my school in the village, and two or three poor old people to look after. My life is not altogether an empty one; but what I do seems so small and trifling in comparison with what I think I should like to do. After all, these may be only the foolish longings of an ignorant girl who has seen little or nothing of the world."

Mr. Bootle came up and claimed Ella's hand for the next dance. The special correspondent's face softened as he looked after her.

"What a sweet creature she is!" he said to himself. "To-morrow I will try to sketch her face from memory."

Philip Cleeve was one of the earliest to leave. He had complained of a severe headache for the last hour, and had scarcely danced at all. A little later Mr. Bootle and Captain Lennox went off arm-in-arm. They had never met before this evening, but they seemed to have taken a mutual liking to one another. When Conroy took his leave, Mrs. Carlyon invited him to call again: and he silently promised himself it should be before Ella Winter's departure for Norfolk. But, as circumstances fell out, it was a promise that he could not keep.

Two o'clock was striking as Mrs. Carlyon sat down on her dressing-room sofa after the departure of her last guest. Taking out her ear-rings, she handed them to her maid, Higson.

"I am glad things passed off nicely," she remarked to Ella, who had stepped in for a few moments' chat. "All the same, I am not sorry it's over," she added, with a sigh of weariness.

"Neither am I," acknowledged Ella. "It would take me a long time to get used to your London hours, Aunt Gertrude."

"That Captain Lennox seems a very pleasant man. Very stylish too; but he-- Higson, what in the world are you fidgeting about?" Mrs. Carlyon broke off to ask.

"I am looking for your jewel-case, ma'am," was the maid's rejoinder; "I can't see it anywhere. Perhaps you have put it away?" she added, turning to her mistress.

"I have neither seen it nor touched it since I dressed for dinner," said Mrs. Carlyon. "It was on the dressing-table then. I dare say you have put it somewhere yourself."

Higson, the patient, knew that she had not, though she made no reply. She continued her search, Ella turning to help her. The maid's face gradually acquired a look of consternation.

"It is certainly not here, aunt," cried Ella.

"What's that, my dear?" asked Mrs. Carlyon, with a start, rousing herself from the half-doze into which she had fallen. "I say that Higson must have forgotten what she did with it."

But Higson had not. She assured her mistress that the jewel-box was left on the dressing-table. At nine o'clock, when she went in to prepare the room for the night, she saw it there, safe and untouched.

Without another word, Mrs. Carlyon set to work herself. The dressing-room had two doors, one of which opened into Mrs. Carlyon's bedroom, while the other opened into the boudoir where the little group had assembled to examine Mr. Conroy's sketches. After searching the dressing-room thoroughly, and convincing herself that the case was not there, the bedroom was submitted to a similar process with a like result.

Mrs. Carlyon grew alarmed. The case had contained jewels of the value of more than three hundred pounds, besides certain souvenirs pertaining to dear ones whom she had lost, which no money could have bought. As a last resource the boudoir was searched, although it was difficult to imagine how the jewel-case could by any possibility have found its way there. Satisfied at length that further search, for the present at all events, was useless, Mrs. Carlyon sat down with despair at her heart and tears in her eyes.

"Are the servants gone to bed yet?" she asked.

Higson thought not. When she came up they were clearing away the refreshments.

"Go and call them," said her mistress, rather sharply. "But don't say what for."

"Higson seems very much put out," observed Ella, when the maid was gone.

"Well she may be," said Mrs. Carlyon. "She is a faithful creature, and has been with me nearly a dozen years. *All* my servants are faithful, and have lived with me more or less a prolonged time," she added emphatically. "I could never suspect one of them; but it is right they should be questioned. I could trust them with all I possess."

The servants filed in, five or six of them, one after another; an expression on each face which seemed to ask, "Why are we wanted here at this uncanny hour?"

In a few quiet sentences Mrs. Carlyon detailed her loss, and questioned each of them in turn as to whether they could throw any light on the affair. One and all denied all knowledge of it: as indeed their mistress had quite expected that they would do. No one save Higson had set foot either in the bedroom or dressing-room since ten o'clock the previous forenoon. There was nothing for it but to let them go back. Higson, who was crying by this time, was told a few minutes later that she too had better go: Mrs. Carlyon would to-night undress herself. The woman went out with her apron to her eyes.

"I shan't get a wink of sleep all this blessed night," she cried with a sob. "Hanging would be too good, ma'am, for them that have robbed you."

Mrs. Carlyon and Ella sat and looked at each other. The uncertainty was growing painfully oppressive. Had there been any strange waiters in the house, they might have been suspected: but, except on some very rare and grand occasion, Mrs. Carlyon employed only her own servants. And those servants were above suspicion.

"Was the door that opens from the dressing-room into the boudoir locked, or otherwise?" asked Ella.

"To my certain knowledge it was locked till past ten o'clock: and I will tell you how I happen to know it," replied Mrs. Carlyon. "Some time after the exhibition of Mr. Conroy's sketches I went into the boudoir and found it empty of everybody except Philip Cleeve; he was lying on the sofa with one of his bad headaches. Thinking that my salts might be of service to him, I came into the dressing-room to get them. I have a clear recollection of finding the door between the two rooms locked then. I unlocked it, and having found the salts, I went back and gave them to Philip; but whether I relocked the door after me is more than I can say. Probably I did not. After a few words to Philip I left him, still lying on the sofa, and did not go near the boudoir again."

A pause ensued. It seemed as if there was nothing more to be said. Not the slightest shadow of suspicion could rest on Philip Cleeve; the idea was preposterous. Both the ladies had known him since he was a boy, and his mother, Lady Cleeve, was one of Mrs. Carlyon's oldest friends. And, that suspicion could attach itself to any of the guests, was equally out of the question. Still, the one strange fact remained, that the casket could not be found.

"We had better go to bed, I think," said Mrs. Carlyon at last, in a fretful voice. "If we sit up all night the case won't come back to us of its own accord."

"I am ready to say with Higson that I shan't get a wink of sleep," remarked Ella, as she rose to obey. "One thing seems quite certain, Aunt Gertrude-- that there must be a thief somewhere."

CHAPTER III.

CAPTAIN LENNOX STARTLED

There were other people beside Mrs. Carlyon who had cause to remember the night of Ella Winter's birthday party.

As already stated, Captain Lennox and Mr. Bootle left the house together. They were walking along, arm-in-arm, smoking their cigars, when whom should they run against but Philip Cleeve, who had bid them goodnight half an hour before.

"Why, Phil, my boy, what are you doing here?" cried Mr. Bootle. "I thought you were off to roost long ago."

"I am taking a quiet stroll before turning in," answered Philip. "I thought the cool night air would do my head good, and I'm happy to say it has."

"Then you can't do better than come along to my hotel with Mr. Bootle," said Lennox. "Let us have one last bottle of champagne together."

Freddy seconded the proposition; and Philip, who seldom wanted much persuasion where pleasure was concerned, yielded after a minute's hesitation. He had come up to London for a few days' holiday, and there was no reason why he should not enjoy himself.

A cab was called, and the three gentlemen presently found themselves at the Captain's rooms. There they sat chatting, and smoking, and drinking champagne, till the clock on the chimney-piece chimed the half hour past two. By this time they had all had more wine than was good for them, Mr. Bootle especially so, while Philip was, perhaps, the coolest of the three.

"We'll see him into a hansom, and then we shall be sure that he will get home all right," whispered Lennox to Philip as they assisted Freddy downstairs.

A hansom being quickly found, Mr. Bootle was safely stowed inside and the requisite instructions given to the driver. Then they all shook hands and bade each other goodnight with a promise to meet again next afternoon.

It was near noon the next day, and Freddy Bootle was still in bed, when some one knocked at his door, and Captain Lennox entered the room, looking well, but lugubrious.

"Not up yet!" he said, in anything but a cheerful voice. "I breakfasted three hours ago."

"My head is like a lump of lead," moaned Freddy, "and my tongue is as dry as a parrot's."

"Have you any soda; and where's your liqueur-case? I'll concoct you a dose that will soon put you right."

"You'll find lots of things in the other room: but Lennox, how fresh you look. You might never have had a headache in your life."

"You are not so well seasoned as I am," returned Captain Lennox. "What business do you suppose has brought me here?"

"Not the remotest idea; unless it be to gaze on the wretched object before you."

"Oh, you'll be well enough in an hour or two. Are you aware that I had my pocket picked of my purse while in your company last night--or, rather, early this morning?"

Mr. Bootle stared at his friend in blank surprise, but said nothing.

"It contained all the cash I had with me," continued the Captain; "and I must ask you to lend me a few pounds to pay my hotel bill and carry me home."

"Was there much in it?"

"A ten-pound note, and some gold and silver."

Mr. Bootle was sitting up in bed by this time, his hands pressed to his head, his eyes fixed intently on the Captain. "By Jove!" he said, at last, and there was no mistaking his tone of utter surprise. "Do you know, Lennox, that your telling me about this brings back something to my mind that I had forgotten till now. I believe my pocket also was picked. I have a vague recollection of not being able to find my watch and chain when I got home this morning, but I tumbled into bed almost immediately, and thought nothing more of the matter till you spoke now. Just hand me my togs and let me have another search."

Mr. Bootle examined his clothes thoroughly; but both watch and chain were gone. The two men looked at each other in dismay. "It was the governor's watch," said Freddy, dismally, "and I am uncommonly sorry it's gone. Bad luck to the scoundrel who took it!"

"You had better get up and have some breakfast, and then we'll go down to Scotland Yard. The police may be able to trace it into the hands of some pawnbroker."

"I shall never see the old watch again," said Mr. Bootle, with a melancholy shake of the head. "And as for breakfast--don't mention the word."

At this juncture, Philip Cleeve came in, looking none the worse for last night's vigil. The story of the double loss was at once poured into his ears by Freddy. Captain Lennox noticed how genuinely surprised he looked.

"*You* lost nothing, I suppose?" asked the Captain, in a grumbling tone, as if he could not get over his own loss.

"Why, no," said Philip, with a laugh. "I had nothing about me worth taking--only a little loose silver and this ancient turnip--a family relic, three or four generations old." As he spoke he drew from his pocket a large old-fashioned silver watch, of the kind our great-grandfathers used to carry, and held it up for inspection. "Almost big enough for a family clock, is it not?" he asked, with another laugh, as he put it away again.

There was silence for a minute or two, Lennox seeming lost in a reverie. Then he turned to Bootle. "Do you recollect at what time during the evening you looked at your watch last?"

"My memory as to what happened during the latter part of the evening is anything but clear," said Freddy. "I seem to have a hazy recollection of pulling out my watch and looking at it when the clock in your room chimed something or other."

"That would be half-past two," interrupted Lennox.

"But I can't be quite sure on the point. How about your purse?--portemonnaie, or whatever it was?"

"As to that, I only know that I missed it first when I came to undress. I might have been relieved of it hours before, or only a few minutes."

"Don't you remember two or three rough-looking fellows hustling past us," asked Philip, "as we stood talking for a minute or two at the street corner just before Bootle got into the cab?"

Lennox shook his head. "I can't say that I recollect the circumstance you speak of," he answered.

"But I recollect the affair quite well," said Philip, positively. "One of the men nearly hustled me into the gutter. Nasty low-looking fellows they were. I think it most likely that they were the pickpockets."

The Captain shrugged his shoulders, remarking that all he knew was that his money was gone; he crossed the room, and began to stare out of the window. Freddy Bootle was looking dreadfully uncomfortable.

"I am sorry that I can't join you fellows at dinner to-day," said Philip. "From a letter I received this morning I find I must get back home at once."

"Oh, nonsense!" both of them interrupted. "That won't do, Cleeve."

"It must do. My mother has written for me. She's ill."

"You can go down the first thing tomorrow," said Captain Lennox.

"A few hours can't make much difference," added Bootle.

Philip shook his head. "When it comes to the mother writing and confessing she is ill--which she seldom will confess--I know she is ill, and that she expects me. Perhaps I'll look in again on my way to the train," added Philip, as he went out. "I have a call or two to make first."

In the course of the day the Captain and Mr. Bootle went down to Scotland Yard and reported their losses: though they both seemed to feel that their doing so was little better than a farce. They dined together afterwards, and went to the theatre.

Next day the Captain's brief visit came to an end, and he travelled back to Norfolk.

The evening clock was striking nine as Captain Lennox reached Nullington station. He secured the solitary fly in waiting, and told the driver to take him to Heron Dyke. Late though it was, he thought he would tell the Squire that his gift had reached Miss Winter safely. What with this robbery and that, it behoved people to be cautious. Dismissing the fly when he reached the gates of Heron Dyke, Captain Lennox took out his cane and a small handbag, and rang at the door.

Everything looked dark about the old house. There was not a glimmer of light anywhere. The shrill clang of the bell broke the deathlike silence rudely. Presently came the sound of footsteps, and then a man's voice could be heard as he grumbled and muttered to himself, while two or three heavy bolts were slowly, and, as it were, reluctantly withdrawn. "It's old Aaron Stone, and he's in a deuce of a temper, as he always is," said the Captain to himself. The great oaken door seemed to groan as it turned on its hinges. It was only opened to the extent of a few inches, and was still held by the heavy chain inside.

"Who are you, and what do you mean by disturbing honest folk at this time o' night?" queried a harsh voice from within.

"I am Captain Lennox. I have just returned from London, and I should like a few words with the Squire, if not too late."

"The Squire never sees anybody at this time o' night. You had better come in the morning, Captain."

"I cannot come in the morning. I have a message for Mr. Denison from his niece, Miss Winter."

"Why couldn't you say so at first?" grumbled the old man. He seemed to hesitate for a moment or two; then he turned on his heel and went slowly away down the echoing corridor; a distant door was heard to shut, and after that all was silence again.

Captain Lennox turned away and whistled a few bars under his breath. The night was cloudy, and few stars were visible. Here and there one of the huge clumps of evergreens, in front of the house, was dimly discernible; and against the background of clouded sky, the black outlines of the seven tall poplars, that stood on the opposite side of the lawn, were clearly defined. A brooding quiet seemed to rest over the whole place, except that every now and then, borne from afar, came the sound of a faint murmurous monotone, at once plaintive and soothing. It was the voice of the incoming tide, as it washed softly up the distant sands.

Captain Lennox shivered, although the night was warm and oppressive. "What a dismal place!" was his thought. "I Would far sooner live in my own pretty little cottage than in this big, rambling, draughty, haunted old house-- and it has a haunted look, if house ever had--and it *is*, if all tales are true. What was that?" he asked himself, with a start. It seemed to him that he had heard the sound of stealthy footsteps behind him. His fingers tightened on his cane, and he peered cautiously around: but nothing was to be seen or heard. Again came the noise of a far-off door, and again the sound of slow, heavy footsteps across the stone-floor of the hall. Next minute the chain was unloosed, and the great door opened a few inches wider. Then was the rugged face and bent form of old Aaron Stone discernible, as he cautiously held the door with one hand, while the other held a lighted lantern.

"You may come in," he said, in ungracious accents. "As you have brought a message from Miss Ella, the Squire will see you; but it's gone nine o'clock, Captain, and he never likes to be kept up past his time--ten."

Captain Lennox stepped inside, and the door behind him was rebolted and chained. The dim light from the lantern flung fantastic shadows on wall and ceiling as Aaron went slowly along, but left other things in semi-darkness. At the end of a passage leading from the opposite side of the hall was a door, which the old man opened with a pass-key, and they turned to the right along a narrower passage, into which several rooms opened. At one of these doors Aaron halted, opened it, and announced Captain Lennox.

The room into which Lennox was ushered, after leaving his handbag and cane outside, was a large apartment, with a sort of sombre stateliness about it which might be imposing, but which was certainly anything but cheerful. Cheerful, indeed, on the brightest day in summer it was hardly possible that this room could be. Its panelled walls were black with age. Here and there a family portrait, dim and faded, and incrusted with the accumulated grime of generations, stared out at you with ghostly eyes from the more ghostly depths of blackness behind it. Whatever colour the ceiling might once have been, it was now one dull pervading hue of dingy brown. Two or three Indian rugs on the floor; a bureau carved with leaves and flowers, from the midst of which queer faces peeped out; two or three tables with twisted legs; an Oriental jar or two, and a few straight-backed chairs, formed, with two exceptions, the sole furniture of the room. The windows were high and narrow, and three in number. They were filled with small lozenge-shaped panes of thick greenish glass, set in lead; through which even the brightest summer sunlight penetrated with a chastened lustre, as though it were half afraid to venture inside. It was night now, and in the silver sconces over the chimney-piece, and in the silver candlesticks on one of the tables, some half-dozen wax-candles were alight; but in that big gloomy room their feeble flame seemed to do little more than make darkness visible. High up in the middle window was the family escutcheon in painted glass, and below it a scroll with the family motto: *What I have, I hold.*

The two exceptions in question were these: a high screen of dark stamped leather, the figures on which, originally gilt, showed nothing more than a patch here and there of their whilom lustre; and a huge chair, which was also covered with the same dark leather. In this chair was seated the Master of Heron Dyke. The screen was drawn up behind him, and although the evening was close on midsummer, in the big open fireplace, in front of which he was sitting, the stump of a tree was slowly burning; crackling and sputtering noisily every now and then, as though defying till the last the flames that were gradually eating it away.

Gilbert Denison sat in this huge leather chair, propped up with cushions, his legs and feet covered with a bear-skin. The reader at first might hardly have believed him to be the fine young fellow he saw in London, sitting by his uncle's death-bed, Gilbert the elder. But forty-five years suffice to change all of us. He was a very tall, lean, gaunt old man now: so lean, indeed, that there seemed to be little more of him than skin and bone. His head was covered with a black velvet skull-cap, underneath which his long white hair straggled almost on his shoulders. He had bold, clearly-cut features, and must, at one time, have been a man of striking appearance. His cheeks had now fallen in, and his long, straight nose looked pinched and sharp. His white eyebrows were thick and heavy, but the eyes below them gleamed out with a strange, keen, crafty sort of intelligence, that was hardly pleasant to see in one so old. He was clad, this evening, in a dressing-gown of thick grey duffel, from the sleeves of which protruded two bony hands, their long fingers just now clutching the arms of the easy-chair as though they never meant to loosen their hold again. Finally, on one lean, yellow finger gleamed a splendid cat's-eye ring, set with brilliants.

Captain Lennox walked slowly forward till he stood close by the invalid's chair: for an invalid Mr. Denison was, and had been for years. The latter spoke first. "So--so! You have got back from town, eh, and brought me a message from my little girl?" said he, looking up at his visitor with sharp, crafty eyes. "I hope that the London smoke and London hours have not quite robbed her of her country roses? But sit down--sit down."

"Miss Winter could hardly look better than when I saw her the day before yesterday," replied Captain Lennox. "She desired me to present her dearest love to you, and to tell you that she would not fail to be back at Heron Dyke on Monday evening next."

"I knew she would be back to her time," chuckled the Squire. "Though, for that matter, she might have stayed another fortnight had she wanted to."

He had a harsh, creaking, high-pitched voice, as though there were some hidden hinges somewhere that needed oiling; and it was curious to note that Aaron Stone's voice, probably from listening to that of his master for so many years, had acquired something of the same harsh, high-pitched tone, only with more of an inherent grumble in it. At a little distance, a person not in the habit of hearing either of them speak frequently, might readily have mistaken one voice for the other.

"I fancy, sir," said the Captain, "that Miss Winter is never so happy as when at Heron Dyke. She strikes me as being one of those exceptional young ladies who care but little for the gaieties and distractions of London life."

"Aye, the girl's been happy enough here, under the old roof-tree of her forefathers. She has been brought up on our wild east coast, and our cold sea winds have made her fresh and rosy. She is not one of your town-bred minxes, who find no happiness out of a ball-room or a boudoir. But she is a child no longer, and girls at her age have sometimes queer fancies and desires, that come and go beyond their own control. There have been times of late when I have fancied my pretty one has moped a little. Maybe, her wings begin to flutter, and to her young eyes the world seems wide and beautiful, and the old nest to grow duller and darker day by day."

His voice softened wonderfully as he spoke thus of Ella. He sat and stared at the burning log, his chin resting on his breast. For the moment he had forgotten that he was not alone.

Captain Lennox waited a minute and then coughed gently behind his hand. The Squire turned his head sharply. "Bodikins! I'd forgotten all about you," he said. "Well, I'm glad you've called to-night, Captain, though if you had come much later I should have been between the blankets. We are early birds at the Dyke. And she was looking well, was she!--forgetting a bit, maybe, the trouble here. You gave my little present safely into her hands, eh?"

"I did not fail to deliver it speedily, as I had promised. Miss Winter will tell you herself how delighted she was with its contents."

The Squire chuckled and rubbed his bony hands. "Ay, ay, she was pleased, was she? I shall have half a dozen kisses for it, I'll be bound."

The Captain rose to go. "I thought you would like to hear of her welfare, Squire, or I should not have intruded on you before tomorrow. And also that I had carried your present to her in safety. London seems full of mysterious robberies just now."

"It's always that; always that. I won't ask you to stay now," added the Squire; "you must drop in and see us another time. There's not much company comes to the Dyke nowadays. But at odd times a friend is welcome, eh? I've been thinking lately that perhaps my pretty one would be more lively if she saw more company: she finds it a bit drear, I fancy, since--since that matter in the winter. You, now, are young, but not too young; you have travelled, and seen the world, and you can talk. So you may call--once in a way, you know, eh--why not?"

As soon as Captain Lennox had gone Aaron came in. One by one, he slowly and with much deliberation extinguished the candles in the sconces over the chimney-piece, but not those on the table. He then proceeded to close and bar the shutters of the three high, narrow windows. It was a whim of Mr. Denison to have the windows of whatever room he might be sitting in left uncurtained and unshuttered till the last moment before retiring for the night. "I hate to sit in a room with its eyes shut," he used to say: and he never would do so if he could help it.

The clatter made by Aaron roused Mr. Denison from the reverie into which he had fallen. He lifted his head and watched Aaron bar the shutters of the last window. "As I drove home this afternoon, master," said Aaron, "I saw two strangers loitering about the park gates. They crossed the stile into the Far Meadow when they saw me, and then they slipped away behind the hedges."

"Ay, ay--spies--spies!" said the Squire. "They are at their old tricks again!--I've felt it for weeks. But we'll cheat them yet, Aaron--yes, we'll cheat them yet. Why, only an hour ago, when it was growing dark, just before you brought in the candles, as I sat looking out of the middle window, all at once I saw a man's face above the garden wall, staring straight into the room. I stared back at it, you may be sure. But at the end of two minutes or so, I could bear the thing no longer, so I up with my stick and shook it at the face, and next moment it was gone."

"I should like to shoot them--and them that send them!" exclaimed Aaron, viciously.

"They'll prowl about more than ever till the next eleven or twelve months have come and gone," said the Squire. "If they could see my coffin carried across the park to the old church, what a merry show that would be for them!--there'd be no more spying here then. That's ten o'clock striking. Put out the other candles and let us go."

Captain Lennox left the hall, carrying his cane and his little bag, and set off homewards. It was a balmy June evening, and the walk through the park would be a pleasant one. As soon as the door was shut behind him he proceeded to light a cigar, and, after crossing the lawn and the old bridge over the moat, he turned to the left and struck into a narrow footpath through the park, which would prove a shorter cut to the high road than the winding carriage-drive. Darkness and silence were around him: the stars gave but little light. He seemed to follow the pathway by instinct rather than by sight. It was a thinner line of grass that wound like a ribbon through the thicker grass of the park. His own footsteps were all but inaudible to him as he walked.

The pathway took a sudden turn round two gnarled thorn-trees, when all at once, and without a moment's warning, Captain Lennox found himself face to face with a dark-hooded figure--hooded and cloaked from head to foot-- which might have sprung out of the ground, so silently and suddenly did it appear to his sight. The Captain, bold man though he was, felt startled, and an involuntary cry escaped his lips. The figure was startled too--it appeared to have been gazing intently at the windows of the house through the branches of the trees--and would have turned to run away. But Captain Lennox took a quiet step forward, and laid his hand upon its shoulder.

"Who are you?--and what are you doing here?" he sternly demanded.

The hood fell back, and in the dim starlight Captain Lennox could just make out the face of a woman, young and pale, her eyes cast pleadingly up to his own.

"Oh, sir, don't hold me!--don't keep me!" was the answer, given in a tone of wailing entreaty, though the voice was one of singular sweetness. "Please let me go!"

"What are you doing here?" he reiterated, still keeping his hold upon her. "What were you peeping at the house for?"

"I am looking for Katherine," whispered the girl. "I come here often to look for her."

"For Katherine!--and who is Katherine?" asked Captain Lennox. But the next moment he remembered the name, as being the one connected with that strange mystery that so puzzled Heron Dyke.

"For my sister," softly repeated the girl. "I do no harm, sir, in coming here to look for her."

"But, my good girl, she is not to be seen, you know; she never will be seen," he remonstrated, a shade of compassion in his tone.

"But I do see her," answered the girl, her voice dropped to so low a pitch that he could scarcely hear it. "I have seen her once or twice, sir; at her own window."

Perhaps Captain Lennox felt a little taken aback at the words. He did not answer.

"People say she must be dead; I know that," went on the speaker, in the same hushed tone. "Even mother says that it must be Katherine's ghost I see. But I think it is herself, sir. I think she is somewhere inside Heron Dyke."

If Captain Lennox felt a shade of something not agreeable creeping over him, he may be excused. The subject altogether bordered on the supernatural.

"My poor girl, had you not better go home and go to bed?" he said, compassionately. "You can do no possible good by wandering about here at this time of night."

"Oh, sir, I must wander; I must find out what has become of her," was the girl's pleading answer. "I can't rest night or day; mother knows I can't. When I go to sleep it is Katherine's voice that wakes me again."

"But----"

"Hark! what was that?" she suddenly cried out, laying her hand lightly, for protection, on the Captain's arm. And he started again, in spite of himself.

"I heard nothing," he said, after listening a moment.

"There it is again; a second scream. There were two screams, you know, sir--her screams--heard that snowy February night."

"But, my good girl, there were no screams to be heard now. It is your imagination. The air is as still as death."

Ere the words were well spoken, the girl was gone. She had vanished silently behind the thorn-trees. And Captain Lennox, after waiting a minute or two, and not feeling any the merrier for the encounter, pursued his walk across the park.

Suddenly, however, as a thought struck him, he turned to look at the windows of the house. They lay in the shade, gloomy and grim, no living person, no light, to be seen in any one of them.

"It is a curious fancy of hers, though," muttered the Captain to himself, as he wheeled round again and went on his way.

CHAPTER IV.

HERON DYKE AND ITS INMATES

The Denisons--or Denzons, as they used formerly to spell their name--were one of the oldest families in that part of Norfolk in which Heron Dyke was situated. They could trace back their descent in a direct line as far as the reign of Henry the Third, but beyond that their pedigree was lost in the mists of antiquity. Who was the first member of the family that settled at Heron Dyke, and how he came by the estate, were moot points which it was hardly likely would ever be satisfactorily cleared up after such a lapse of time. The Denisons had never been more than plain country squires. Several female members of the family had married people of title, but none of the males had ever held anything more than military rank. James the Second had offered a barony to the then head of the family, and the second George a baronetcy to the Squire of that day, but both offers had been respectfully declined.

No family in the county was better known, either by name or reputation, than the Denisons--the "Mad Denisons," as they were often called, and had been called any time these three hundred years. Not that any of them had ever been charged with lunacy, or had been shut up in a madhouse; but they had always been known as an excitable, eccentric race, full of "queer notions," addicted to madcap pranks and daredevil feats, such as seldom failed to astonish and sometimes frighten their quiet neighbours, and had long ago earned for them the unenviable sobriquet mentioned above.

A Gilbert Denison it was who, in the reign of William and Mary, wagered a hundred guineas that on a certain fifth of November he would have a bigger bonfire than his near friend and neighbour, Colonel Duxberry. A bigger bonfire he certainly had, for with his own hand he fired three of the largest hayricks on the farm, and so won the wager.

A later Squire Denison it was who, when his father died and he should have come into the estate, was nowhere to be found, and did not turn up till two years afterwards. He had quarrelled with his parents and run away from home; and he was ultimately found earning his living as bare-back rider in a country circus. He it was who, when his friend the clown called upon him a year or two later to beg the loan of a sovereign, dressed the man up in one of his own suits and introduced him to his guests at table as a distinguished traveller just returned from the East. Old Lord Fosdyke, who sat next the clown at dinner and was much taken with him, made a terrible to-do when he was told of the hoax that had been played off upon him: ever afterwards he refused to speak or recognise Mr. Denison in any way.

Two other heads of the family lost their lives in duels; one of them by the hand of his dearest friend, with whom he had had a difference respecting the colour of a lady's eyebrows: the other by a stranger, with whom he had chosen to pick a quarrel "just for the fun of the thing." There was an old distich well known to the country-folk for twenty miles round Heron Dyke, which sufficiently emphasised the popular notion of the family's peculiarities. It ran as under:

"Whate'er a Denzon choose to do,
  Need ne'er surprise nor me nor you."

The existing mansion at Heron Dyke was the third which was known to have been built on the same site, or in immediate proximity to it. The present house bore the date 1616, the one to which it was the successor having been destroyed by fire. There was a tradition in the family that the whilom lord of Heron Dyke set fire to the roof-tree of the old mansion with his own hand, hoping by such summary method to exorcise the ghost of a girl dressed in white and having a red spot on her breast, which would persist in rambling through the upper chambers of the house during that weird half-hour when the daylight is dying, and night has not yet come. He had lately brought home his bride, and the young wife vowed that she would go back to her mother unless the ghost were got rid of. It is to be presumed that the means adopted proved effectual, since there seems to be no further record of the girl in white ever having put in an appearance afterwards.

The present mansion of Heron Dyke formed three sides of an oblong square. A low, broad, lichen-covered wall made up the fourth side, just outside of which ran the moat, a sluggish stream some ten or dozen feet broad, spanned by an old stone bridge grey with age. The house, which was but two stories high, was built of the black flints so common in that part of the country, set in some sort of cement which age had hardened to the consistency of stone. Here and there the dull uniformity of the thick walls was relieved by diaper-patterned pilasters of faded red brick. The high, narrow, lozenge-paned windows were set in quaintly carved mullions of reddish freestone, the once sharp outlines of which were now blurred with age. The steep, high-pitched roof was covered with blue-black tiles which at one time had been highly glazed, but the rains and snows of many winters had dimmed their brightness, while in summer many-coloured mosses found lodgment in their crevices and patched them here and there with beauty. The tall, twisted chimneys of deep-red brick lent their warmth and colouring to the picture.

There were dormer windows in the roofs of the two wings, but none in the main building itself. The grand entrance was reached by a flight of broad, shallow steps, crowned with a portico that was supported by five Ionic columns: a somewhat incongruous addition to a house that otherwise was thoroughly English in all its aspects. In front of the house was a large oval lawn clumped with evergreens and surrounded by a carriage-drive. The stables and domestic offices were hidden away at the back of the house, where also were the kitchen-garden, the orchard, and a walled-in flower garden, into which looked the windows of Mr. Denison's favourite sitting-room. Just inside the low, broad wall, that bounded the moat, grew seven tall poplars, known to the cottagers and simple fisher-folk thereabouts, as "The Seven Maidens of Heron Dyke."

The park was not of any great extent, the distance from the moat to the lodge-gates on the high-road to Nullington being little more than half a mile. But it was well wooded, and had nothing formal about it, and such as it was it seemed a fitting complement to the old house that looked across its pleasant glades. The house was built in a sheltered hollow not quite half a mile from the sea. It was protected on the north by a shelving cliff that was crowned with a lighthouse. Behind it the ground rose gradually and almost imperceptibly for a couple of miles, till the little town of Nullington was reached. Not far from the southern corner of the Hall, was an artificial hillock of considerable size and some fifty or sixty feet in height, which was thickly planted with larches. The park in front of the house swept softly upward to its outermost wall. Beyond that, was a protecting fringe of young larches and scrub-wood, then the ever-shifting sand-dunes, and, last of all, the cold grey waters of the North Sea. For miles southward the land was almost as flat as a billiard-table. The fields were divided by dykes which had been dug for drainage purposes, with here and there a fringe of pollard willows to break the dead level of monotony. The sea was invisible from the lower windows of the Hall, but there was a fine view of it from the dormer windows in the north wing; and here Ella Winter had had a room fitted up especially for herself. Had you ever slept at Heron Dyke on a winter night, when a strong landward breeze was blowing, you would have been hushed to rest by one of nature's most majestic monotones. When you lay down and when you arose, you would have had in your ears the thunderous beat of countless thousands of white-lipped angry waves on the long level reaches of sand, that stretched away southward for miles as far as the eye could reach.

When Gilbert Denison, uncle to the present Squire of Heron Dyke, died from the results of an accident, at his lodgings in Bloomsbury Square, and when the strange nature of his will came to be noised abroad, there was no lack of ill-advisers, who did their best to induce the youthful heir to contest the validity of the dead man's last testament. But young Gilbert knew that his uncle had never been saner in his life than when he planned that particular proviso; besides which, he was far too proud of his family name to drag the will of a Denison through the mire of the law courts. His uncle, who had always been looked upon as a sober, thrifty, bucolic-minded sort of man, had not failed to redeem the family reputation for eccentricity at the last moment, and young Gilbert had an idea that it was just the sort of thing he himself would have been likely to do under similar circumstances.

To the surprise of his boon companions, he quietly accepted the situation thus forced upon him, and determined to make the best of it. After giving a farewell symposium to the friends who had so kindly helped him to sow his wild oats, London saw him no more for several years. He settled down at Heron Dyke, and became as staid and sober a specimen of a country gentleman as a Denison was ever likely to become. His somewhat shattered constitution was now nursed with all due care and tenderness. If it were in the power of man to defeat that last hateful clause in his uncle's will, he was the man to do it.

"He will be sure to choose a wife before long," said all the anxious matrons in the neighbourhood, who had eligible daughters waiting to be mated. But Gilbert Denison did nothing of the kind. Years went by. He became a middle-aged man, then an elderly man, and all hope of his ever changing his bachelor condition gradually died out. There was a constantly floating rumour in the neighbourhood of a romantic attachment and a disappointment when he was young; but it might be nothing more than an idle story. It was even said that the lady had jilted him in favour of his cousin, and that there would have been bloodshed between the two men had not the other Gilbert hurried away with his young wife to Italy.

It was this other Gilbert, or his descendants, who would come in for the Heron Dyke estates, should the present Squire not live to see his seventieth birthday. There was no love lost between the senior and junior branches of the family. The estrangement begun in early life only widened with years. Its continuance, if not its origin, was probably due to the Squire's hard and unforgiving disposition. The other side had more than once made friendly overtures to the head of the house: but the Squire would have none of them. He hated the whole "vile crew," root and stump, he said; and if any one of them ever dared to darken his threshold, he vowed that he would shoot him without compunction. It was Squire Denison's firm and fixed belief that the spies sometimes seen around his house--for spies he declared them to be-- were emissaries of his relatives, sent to see whether he was not likely to die before the all-important birthday.

We made the Squire's acquaintance at his interview with Captain Lennox, after the return of the latter from London. His sixty-ninth birthday was just over. Could he but live eleven months more, all would be well. Ella Winter, in that case, would be heiress to all he had to leave, for he should will it to her; and his hated cousin, and his cousin's family, would be left out in the cold, as they deserved to be. As everybody knew, the Squire had been more or less of an invalid for many years; but latterly his complaint had assumed a rather alarming character, and there were weeks together when he never crossed the threshold of his own rooms. His disorder was a mortal one--one that would most certainly carry him off at no very distant date--but that was a fact known to himself and Dr. Spreckley alone.

For the last twenty years the Squire had not kept up an establishment at the Hall in accordance with his income and position in the county. There was Aaron Stone, his faithful old body-servant and major-domo, and Aaron's wife, who was almost as old as he was. There was the old couple's handsome grandson, Hubert, who was the Squire's steward, bailiff, gamekeeper, and sometimes secretary and companion. There were the gardener and his wife at the lodge on the Nullington road. When to these were added a coachman, a stable-boy, and two or three women-servants, the whole of the establishment was told. Mr. Denison had not given a dinner-party for years; or, for the matter of that, gone to one. Now and then an old acquaintance-- such as the vicar, or Sir Peter Dockwray, or Colonel Townson--would drop in unceremoniously, and take the chance of whatever there happened to be for dinner; but beyond such casual visitants, very little company was kept.

Mr. Denison had been compelled to give up horse-exercise some few years ago. He took his airings in a lumbering, old-fashioned brougham, which might have been stylish and handsome once. Very often nothing occupied the shafts but a grey mare, that was nearly as lumbering as the vehicle itself. Old Aaron could get its best paces out of it when he drove it in the dog-cart to Nullington market and back. Ella Winter had a young chestnut filly for riding, powerful yet gentle, for which her uncle had given quite a fancy price. Another horse in the Squire's stables was a big, serviceable hack, which Hubert Stone looked upon as being for his sole use; indeed, no one but himself ever thought of mounting it. He rode it here and there when about the Squire's business; and sometimes, perhaps, when about his own. Better than all else he liked to accompany Ella when she went out riding. He would be dressed somewhat after the style of a gentleman farmer, in cut-away coat, buckskins, and top-boots. He did not ride by the side of Ella as an equal would have done, nor yet so far behind her as a groom. Many were the comments passed by the gossips of Nullington when they encountered Miss Winter and her handsome attendant cantering along the country roads, or quiet lanes that led to nowhere in particular.

Mr. Denison was well seconded in his saving propensities by his old servant, Aaron Stone. Aaron was born on the Heron Dyke estate, as had been his ancestors before him for two hundred years. Thus it fell out that, at the age of nineteen, he was appointed by the late Squire to attend his nephew when he set out on the Grand Tour, and from that day to the present he had never left him. There were many points of similarity in the tempers and dispositions of master and man. Both of them were obstinate, cross-grained men, with strong wills of their own, and both of them were inclined to play the small tyrant as far as their opportunities would allow. They grumbled at each other from January till December, but were none the less true friends on that account. No other person dare say to the Squire a tithe of the things that Aaron said with impunity, and probably no other servant would have put up with Mr. Denison's wayward humours and variable temper as Aaron did. Twenty times a year the Squire threatened to discharge his old servant as being lazy, wasteful, and good-for-nothing; and a month seldom passed without Aaron vowing that he would pack up his old hair trunk, and never darken the doors of Heron Dyke again. But neither of them meant what he said.

Aaron's wife, Dorothy, had been a Nullington girl, and had heard people talk about the Denisons of Heron Dyke ever since she could remember anything. She was now sixty-five years old: a little, withered, timid woman, slightly deaf, and very much in awe of her husband. She believed in dreams and omens, and was imbued with all sorts of superstitious fancies local to the neighbourhood and to the Hall. Perhaps her deafness had something to do with her reticence of speech, for she was certainly a woman of few words, who went about her duties in a silent, methodical way, and did not favour strangers.

One son alone had blessed the union of Aaron and Dorothy. He proved to be something of a wild spark, and ran away from home before he was one-and-twenty. Subsequently he joined a set of strolling players, and a year or two later he married one of the company. The young lady whom he made his wife was reported to come of a good family, and, like himself, was said to have run away from home. Anyhow, they did not live long to enjoy their wedded happiness. Four years later the little boy, Hubert, fatherless and motherless, was brought to Heron Dyke, and then it was that Aaron Stone learnt for the first time that he had a grandson.

The Squire was pleased with the lad's looks, and took pity on his forlorn condition. He was sent to Easterby, and brought up by one of the fishermen's wives, and when he was old enough he was put to a good school, Mr. Denison paying all expenses. He always spent his holidays at the Hall, and there it was, when he was about twelve years old, that he first saw Ella, who was his junior by two years. Children, as a rule, think little of the differences of social rank; at all events, Ella did not, and she and handsome, bright-eyed Hubert soon became great friends. Mr. Denison, if he noticed the intimacy, did not disapprove of it. They were but children, and no harm could come of it; and perhaps it was as well that Ella should have some one with her besides Nero, the big retriever, when she went for her lonely rambles along the shore, or gathering nuts and blackberries in the country lanes. This pleasant companionship--both pleasant and dangerous to Hubert, young though he still was--was renewed and kept up every holiday season till the boy was sixteen. Then all at once there came a great gap. Ella was sent abroad to finish her education, and although she saw her uncle several times in the interim, Hubert, as it happened, saw no more of her till she came home for good at nineteen years of age. But before this came about, Hubert's own career in life had been settled: at least, for some time to come. When the boy was seventeen the Squire decided that he had had enough schooling, and that it was time for him to set about earning his living. How he was to set about it was apparently a point that required some consideration; meanwhile, the boy stayed on at Heron Dyke. He was a bold rider and a good shot. He wrote an excellent hand, and was quick at figures. In fact, he was an intelligent, teachable young fellow, who had made good use of his opportunities at school: moreover, he could keep his temper well under control when it suited him to do so; and, little by little, the Squire began to find him useful in many ways. He himself was growing old, and Aaron got more stupid every year that he lived. By-and-by nothing more was said about Hubert having to earn a living elsewhere. He relieved the Squire of many duties that had become irksome to him; and when a man of his years has once dropped a burden he rarely cares to pick it up again. In short, by the time Hubert was twenty years old he had made himself thoroughly indispensable to the Squire.

No one but Hubert himself ever knew with what a fever of unrest he awaited the coming home of Ella Winter. Had she forgotten him? Would she recognise him after all these years? How would she greet him? He tormented himself with a thousand vain questions. He knew now that he loved her with all the devotion of a deeply passionate heart.

Miss Winter came at last. The moment her eyes rested on Hubert she recognised him, changed though he was. She came up to him at once, and held out her hand.

"When I see so many faces about me that I remember, then I know that I am at home," she said, looking into his eyes with that sweetly serious look of hers.

Hubert touched her hand, blushed, and stammered; although, as a rule, there were few young men more self-possessed than he was. At the same moment a chill ran through him. His heart seemed as if it must break. The Ella of his day-dreams--the bright-eyed, sunny-haired little maiden, who had treated him almost like a brother, who had grasped his wrist when she leaped across the runlets in the sands, who had imperiously ordered him to drag down the tall branches of the nut-trees till the fruit was within her reach--had vanished from his ken for ever. In her stead stood Miss Winter, a strangely-beautiful young lady, whose face was familiar and yet unfamiliar. As he saw and recognised this, he saw, too, and recognised for the first time, the impassable gulf that divided them. She was a lady, the daughter of an ancient house: he was not a gentleman, and nothing could ever make him one, at least in her eyes, or in the eyes of the world to which she belonged. He was a son of the soil. He was Gurth the swineherd, and she was the Lady Rowena. What folly, what madness, to love one so utterly beyond his reach!

CHAPTER V.

AN UNEXPECTED VISITOR

"You must go round to the side-door if you have any business here," cried a shrill, angry, quavering voice, in answer to the loud knocking of a stranger at the main entrance of Heron Dyke.

Edward Conroy--for he it was--could not at first make out where the voice came from, but when he stepped from under the portico and glanced upward, he saw a withered face protruded from one of the upper windows, and a skinny hand and arm pointing in the direction of a door which he now noticed for the first time in a corner of the right wing. For the first time, too, he saw that the grim old door at which he had been knocking looked as if it had not been opened for years, and that the knocker itself was rusty from disuse. Even the steps that led up to the portico were falling into disrepair, and through the cracks and crevices tiny tufts of grass and patches of velvety moss showed themselves here and there.

Conroy descended the steps slowly, and then turned to take another look at the grey old house, which he had never seen before to-day. The first view of it, as he crossed the bridge over the moat, had not impressed him favourably. But now that he looked at it again, the quaint formality of its lines seemed to please him better. It might have few pretensions to architectural dignity; but, with the passage of years, there had come to it a certain harmoniousness such as it had never possessed when it was new. Summer sun and winter rain had not been without their effect upon it. They had toned down the hardness of its original outlines: its coldness seemed less cold, its formality not so formal, as they must once have seemed. It was slowly mellowing in the soft, sweet air of antiquity.

He noticed, as he walked along the front of the house from the main entrance to the side-door, that the entire range of windows on the ground floor had their shutters fastened, and those of the upper floor their blinds drawn down. His heart chilled for a moment as the thought struck him that some one might perhaps be lying dead inside the house. But then he reflected that he should surely have heard such a thing spoken of at the village inn, where he had slept last night. Was it not, rather, that the house had always the same shut-up look that it wore to-day?

Conroy knocked at the side-door, a heavy door also, and was answered by the loud barking of a dog. After waiting for what seemed an intolerable time, he heard footsteps in the distance, which slowly drew nearer. The door was unbolted, and opened as far as the chain inside would permit. Through this opening peered forth the crabbed, wizened face of an old man--of a man with a pointed chin, and a long nose, and eyes that were full of suspicion and ill-humour.

"And what may be your business at Heron Dyke?" he demanded, in a harsh, querulous voice, after a look that took in the stranger from head to foot.

"Be good enough to give this card to Mr. Denison, and if he can spare two minutes----"

"He won't see any strangers without he knows their business first," interrupted the old man brusquely, as he turned the card to the light that was streaming through the open doorway into the dim corridor in which he stood, and read the name printed on it. "Never heard of you before," he added. "Maybe you are a spy--a mean, dastardly spy," he continued, after a pause, still eyeing the young man suspiciously from under his thick white eyebrows.

"A spy! No, I am not a spy. Have you any spies in these parts?"

"Lots of them."

"And what do they come to spy out?"

"That's none of your business, sir, so long as you're not one--though that has to be proved," answered the crusty old man, as he went away with the card, leaving Conroy outside.

He turned, and began to pace the gravelled pathway in front of the door.

"Is my sweet princess here, I wonder, and shall I succeed in seeing her?" he said to himself. "Very like a wild-goose chase, this errand of mine. To see her once in London for a couple of hours--to fall in love with her then and there--to come racing down to this out-of-the-world spot, weeks afterwards, on the bare possibility of seeing her again--when she probably remembers no more of me than she does of any other indifferent stranger--what can that be but the act of a----"

Light footsteps were coming swiftly down the stone corridor. Conroy's face flushed, and a strange eager light leapt into his eyes. There was a rustle of garments, then the heavy chain dropped, the door swung wide on its hinges, and Ella Winter stood revealed to Conroy's happy gaze.

His card was in her hand. She glanced from it to his face, and, a momentary blush mounting to her cheek, she advanced a step or two, and held out her hand.

"Mr. Conroy," she said, "I have not forgotten your sketches. Or you either," she added, as if by an after-thought, a smile playing round her lips by this time, coming and going like spring sunshine.

She led the way in, and he followed. The long, flagged corridor, with its dim light, struck him with a chill, after coming out of the bright air. Ella entered a small, oak-panelled room, plainly and heavily furnished, and invited Mr. Conroy to sit down.

"We live mostly at the back of the house," she observed. "My uncle prefers the rooms to those in front."

"It is a grand old house," answered Conroy. "And what might it not be made!" he added to himself.

"You received your portfolio of sketches back safely, Mr. Conroy, I hope. My aunt left them at your address that day when we went out for our drive."

"Did you indeed leave them? Were you so good?"

"Sketches such as those are too valuable to be trusted to the chance of loss," said Ella.

"I was so very sorry not to call again on Mrs. Carlyon, as I had promised," he continued, "but the next day but one I had to leave town. I wonder what she thought of me?"

"I don't think she thought at all," replied Ella, ingenuously--"though she would, I am sure, have been glad to see you. Aunt Gertrude was too full of her loss in those days to notice who visited her. On the evening of the party she lost her jewels."

"Lost her jewels!" exclaimed Conroy. "Do you mean those she wore?"

"No, no. Her casket of jewels was stolen from her dressing-room. Some of them were very valuable. The case was left on her dressing-table, and it disappeared during the evening."

"Was the case itself stolen?"

"We thought so that night, but the next morning, when the housemaids were sweeping her boudoir--the room in which we looked at your sketches, if you remember--they found the case on the floor, ingeniously hidden behind the window-curtain."

"Empty?"

"Oh, of course. The thief had taken the contents and left the case. Aunt Gertrude can hear nothing of them."

"I hope and trust she will find them," was Mr. Conroy's warm answer. And then he went on, after a perceptible pause: "I think you know already, Miss Winter, that I am connected with the Press. The world being quiet just now, my employers, having nothing better for me to do, have found a very peaceful mission for me for the time being. They have sent me into this part of the country to take sketches of different old mansions and family seats, and I am here to-day to seek Mr. Denison's permission to make a couple of drawings of Heron Dyke."

Ella hesitated for a moment or two, toying nervously with Conroy's card, which she still held. Then she spoke:

"My uncle is a confirmed invalid, Mr. Conroy, and very much of a recluse. Strangers, or indeed acquaintances whom he has not met for a long time, are unwelcome to him, even when there is no need for him to see them personally. Whether he will see you, or grant you the permission you ask for, without seeing you, is more than I can tell. I will, however, try my best to induce him to do so."

"Thank you very much," said Conroy. "I certainly should like to take some sketches of this old house: but, rather than put Mr. Denison out of the way, or cause the slightest annoyance in the matter, I will forego----"

"Certainly not," Ella hastily interrupted: "at least, until I have spoken to my uncle. If he would but see you it might rouse him from the lethargy that seems to be gradually creeping over him, and would do him good. To receive more visitors would be so much better for him! You will excuse me for a few minutes, will you not?"

"What a life for this fair young creature to lead!" Conroy said to himself as soon as she was gone. "To be shut up in this gloomy old house with a querulous hypochondriac who suspects an enemy in every stranger and dreads he knows not what; but it seems to me that women can endure things that would drive a man crazy. Would that I were the knight to rescue her from this wizard's grasp, and take her out into the sweet sunlight!"

He stood gazing out of the window, tapping the panes lightly with his fingers and smiling to himself, lost in dreams.

"My uncle will see you," said Ella, as she re-entered the room.

"Thank you for your kind intervention."

"He is in one of his more gracious moods to-day; but you must be careful not to contradict him if you wish to obtain his sanction to what you require. And now I will show you to his room."

After traversing two or three flagged passages, Conroy was ushered into a room which might have been an enlarged copy of the one he had just left. It was the same room in which Captain Lennox's interview took place on the night of his return from London. Aaron Stone was coming out as Conroy went in. The old man greeted him with a queer, sour look, and some uncomplimentary remark, muttered to himself. Then he went out, and banged the heavy door noisily behind him.

"S--s--s--s! That confounded door again!" exclaimed a rasping, high-pitched voice from behind the screen at the farther end of the room. "Will that old rapscallion never remember that I have nerves? Ah--ha! if I could but cuff him as I used to do!" added the Squire, breaking off with a fit of coughing.

Ella held up a warning finger, and waited without moving till all was quiet again. She then glided across the polished, uncarpeted floor, and passed in front of the screen. Conroy waited in the background.

"I have brought Mr. Conroy to see you, Uncle Gilbert--the gentleman who wants to take some sketches of the Hall," said Ella, in tones a little louder than ordinary.

"And who gave you leave, young lady, to introduce any strangers here? You know--"

"You yourself gave me leave, uncle, not many minutes ago," she quietly interposed. "You said that you would see Mr. Conroy."

"Did I, child?"

"Certainly you did."

"Then my memory must be failing me faster than I thought it was." Here came a deep sigh, followed by a moment or two of silence. "You are right, Ella. I remember it now. Let us see what this bold intruder is like."

Conroy stepped forward in front of the screen, and saw before him the Master of Heron Dyke. He looked to-day precisely as he had looked that evening, now several weeks ago, when Captain Lennox called at the Hall. It might be that his face was a little thinner and more worn, but that was the only difference.

"So! You are the young jackanapes who wants to sketch my house--eh?" said Mr. Denison, as he peered into Conroy's face with eager, suspicious eyes. "How do I know that you are not a spy--a vile spy?" He ground out the last word from beneath his teeth, and craned his long neck forward so as to bring it closer to Conroy's face.

"Do I look like a spy, sir?" asked Conroy calmly, as he went a pace nearer to the old man's chair.

"What have looks to do with it? There's many a false heart beneath a fair-seeming face. Aye, many--many." He spoke the last words as if to himself, and when he had ended he sat staring out of the window like one who had become suddenly oblivious of everything around him. His lips moved, but no sound came from them.

Mr. Denison's reverie was broken by the entrance of Aaron with letters and newspapers. Then the Squire turned to Conroy. "So you're not a spy, eh? Well, I don't know that you look like one. But pray what can there be about a musty tumble-down old house, like this, that you should want to make a sketch of it?"

"The Denisons are one of the oldest families in Norfolk. Surely, sir, some account of the home of such a family would interest many people."

"And how come you to know so much about the Denisons?" shrewdly asked the Squire. "But sit down. It worries me to see people standing at my elbow."

"Such knowledge is a part of my stock-in-trade," said Conroy, as he took a chair. "I have not only to make the sketches, but to tell the public all about them. Both in Burke and the 'County History' I have found many interesting particulars of the old family whose home is at Heron Dyke."

"So--so! And pray, young sir, what other houses in the county have you sketched before you found your way here?"

"None; I have come to you, sir, before going anywhere else."

"Well said, young man. The county can boast of finer houses by the score, but what are the families who live in them? Mushrooms--mere mushrooms in comparison with the Denisons. We might have been ennobled centuries ago had we chosen to accept a title. But the Denisons always thought themselves above such gewgaws."

"Was it not to the same purport, sir, that Colonel Denison answered James the Second when his Majesty offered him a patent of nobility on the eve of the Battle of the Boyne?"

"Ah--ha! your reading has been to some purpose," said the old man, with a dry chuckle. "That's the colonel's portrait over there in the left-hand corner. They used to tell me that I was something like him when I was a young spark."

Evidently he was pleased. He rubbed his lean, chilly fingers together, and fell into another reverie. Conroy glanced round. Ella was sitting at her little work-table busy with her crewels. What a sweet picture she made in the young man's eyes as she sat there in her grey dress, with the rich coils of her chestnut hair bound closely round her head, and an agate locket set in gold suspended from her neck by a ribbon, in which was a portrait of her dead mother. Not knowing that Conroy was gazing at her, her eyes glanced up from her work and encountered his. Next moment the long lashes hid them again, but the sweet carnation in her cheeks betrayed that she had been taken unawares.

Then Gilbert Denison spoke again. "There's something about you, young man," he said, "that seems to wake in my mind an echo of certain old memories which I thought were dead and buried for ever. Whether it's in your voice, or your eyes, or in the way you carry your head, or in all of them together, I don't know. Very likely what I mean exists only in my own imagination: I sometimes think I'm getting into my dotage. What do you say your name is?" he asked abruptly.

"Conroy, sir. Edward Conroy."

Mr. Denison shook his head. "I never knew any family of that name."

"The Conroys have been settled in North Devon for the last three hundred years."

"Never heard of 'em. But that's no matter. As I said before, there's something about you that comes home to me and that I like, though I'll be hanged if I know what it is, and I've no doubt I'm an old simpleton for telling you as much. Anyhow, you may take what sketches of the place you like. You have my free permission for that. And if you're not above dining off boiled mutton--we are plain folk here now--you may find your way back to this room at five sharp, and there will be a knife and fork ready for you. Why not?"

The interview was over. Ella conducted Conroy into another room, and then rang the bell. "There must be some magic about you," she said, with a smile, "to have charmed my uncle as you have. You don't know what a rarity it is for him to see a fresh face at Heron Dyke."

Aaron Stone answered the bell, Ella gave Conroy into his charge, with instructions to show him all that there was to be seen, and to allow him to sketch whatever he might choose. The old man received this with a bad grace. He had become so thoroughly imbued with the fear of spies and what they might do, that no courtesy was left in him. Growling something under his breath about strangers on a Friday always bringing ill-luck, he limped away to fetch his bunch of keys.

"What a capital subject for an etching," thought Conroy, as he looked after the old man.

When five o'clock struck, Conroy shut up his sketch-book and retraced his way to Mr. Denison's room. The dinner was almost as homely as the host had divined that it would be. But if the viands were plain, the wine was superexcellent, and as Conroy could see that he was expected to praise it, he did not fail to do so. A basin of soup, followed by a little jelly and a glass of Madeira, formed Mr. Denison's dinner. His bodily weakness was evidently very great. It seemed to Conroy that the man was upheld and sustained more by his indomitable energy of will than by any physical strength he might be possessed of. "Heron Dyke will want a new master before long," was Conroy's unspoken thought, as he looked at the long-drawn, cadaverous face before him.

Ella would have left the room when the cloth was drawn, but her uncle bade her stay; for which Conroy thanked him inwardly. The young artist quickly found that if the evening were not to languish, perhaps end in failure, he must do the brunt of the talking himself. Mr. Denison was no great talker at the best of times, and Ella, from some cause or another, was more reserved than usual; so Conroy plunged off at a tangent, and did his best to interest his hearers with an account of his experiences in Paris during the disastrous days of the Commune. As Desdemona of old was thrilled by the story of Othello's adventures, so was Ella thrilled this evening. Even Mr. Denison grew interested, and for once let his mind wander for a little while from his own interests and his own concerns.

As they sat thus, the September evening slowly darkened. The candles were never lighted till the last moment. Conroy sat facing the windows which opened into the private garden at the back of the Hall. The boundary of this garden was an ivy-covered wall about six feet high. A low-browed door in one corner gave access to the kitchen-garden, beyond which was the orchard, and last of all a wide stretch of park. There were flowers in the borders round the garden wall, but opposite the windows grew two large yews, whose sombre foliage clouded much of the light that would otherwise have crept in through the diamond-paned windows, and made more gloomy still an apartment which, even on the brightest of summer days, never looked anything but cheerless and cold. On this overcast September eve the yew-trees outside blackened slowly, and seemed to draw the darkness down from the sky. Aaron came in at last with candles, and while he was disposing them Conroy rose, crossed to one of the windows, and stood looking out into the garden. It was almost dark by this time. While looking thus, he suddenly saw the figure of a man emerge from behind one of the yews, stare intently into the room for a moment, and then vanish behind the other yew. Conroy was startled. Was there, then, really truth in the Squire's assertion that spies were continually hovering round the Hall? Somehow he had deemed it nothing more than the hallucination of a sick man's fancy.

With what object could spies come to Heron Dyke? It was a mystery that puzzled Conroy. He crossed over to Ella and told her in a low voice what he had seen. She looked up with a startled expression in her eyes.

"Don't say a word about it to my uncle," she whispered. "It would only worry him, and could do no good. Both he and Aaron often assert that they see strange people lurking about the house; but I myself have never seen anyone."

The Squire began to talk again, and nothing more passed. When Conroy rose to take his leave, his host held his hand and spoke to him cordially.

"You will be in the neighbourhood for some days, you tell us, Mr. Conroy. If you have nothing better to do on Tuesday than spend a few hours with a half-doited old man and a country lassie, try and find your way here again. Eh, now?"

This, nothing loth, Conroy promised to do; the more so as Ella's needle was suspended in mid-air for a moment while she waited to hear his answer. Conroy's eyes met hers for an instant as she gave him her hand at parting, but she was on her guard this time, and nothing was to be read there.

He had not gone many steps from the house when there was a rustle amidst the trees he was passing; and a young and well-dressed man, so far as Mr. Conroy could see, who had been apparently peering through an opening in the trees, walked quickly away.

"He was watching the house," said Mr. Conroy to himself. "One of the spies, I suppose. What on earth is it that they want to find out?"

Dull enough felt Ella after Conroy's departure.

"I'll get a book," she said, shaking off her thoughts, which had turned on the man Conroy had seen behind the yew-tree: and she went to a distant room in search of one. Coming back with it, she saw the two housemaids, Martha and Ann, standing at the foot of the stairs which led up to the north wing. One of them held a candle, the other clung to her arm; both their faces were wearing an unmistakable look of terror.

"What is the matter?" she asked, going towards them.

"We've just heard something, Miss Ella," whispered Ann. "One of the bedroom-doors up there has just shut with a loud bang."

"And it sounded like the door of *her* room," spoke the other from her pale and frightened lips. "Miss Ella, I am *sure* it was."

"The door of whose room?" asked Miss Winter sharply, her own heart beating fast.

"Of Katherine's," answered both the maids together.

For a moment Ella could not command herself.

"What business had you in this part of the house at all?" she questioned, after a pause.

"Mrs. Stone sent us after her spectacles," explained Ann. "She left them in your sitting-room, ma'am, when she was up there seeing to the curtains this afternoon. She sent us, Miss Ella; she'd not go up herself at dark for the world."

"Did she send both of you?" was the almost sarcastic question.

"Ma'am, she knows neither one of us would dare to go alone."

"You are a pair of silly, superstitious girls," rebuked Miss Winter. "What is there in the north wing to frighten you, more than in any other part of the house? I am surprised at you; at you, Ann, especially, knowing as I do how sensibly your mother brought you up."

"I can't help the feeling, miss, though I do strive against it," said Ann, with a half sob. "I know it's wrong, but I can't help myself turning cold when I have to come into this part of the house after dark."

"We hear noises in the north wing as we don't hear elsewhere," said Martha, shivering. "Miss Ella, it is true--if anything ever was true in this world. It was the door of her room we heard just now--loud enough too. Just as if the wind had blown it to, or as if somebody had shut it in a temper."

"There is hardly enough wind this evening to stir a leaf," reproved their young mistress. "And you know that every door in the north wing is locked outside, except that of my sitting-room."

"No, Miss Ella, there's not enough wind, and the doors is locked, as you say; but we heard one of 'em bang, for all that, and it sounded like her door," answered Martha, with respectful persistency.

Ella looked at the young women. Could she cure them of this foolish fear, she asked herself--or, at least, soften it?

"Come with me, both of you," she said, taking the candle into her hand, and leading the way up the great oaken staircase.

Clinging to each other, the servants followed. This, the north wing, was the oldest part of the house. Here and there a stair creaked beneath their footsteps; at every corner there were fantastic shadows, that seemed to lie in wait and then spring suddenly out. The squeaking of a mouse and the pattering of light feet behind the wainscot made the girls start and tremble; but Ella held lightly on her way till the corridor that ran along the whole length of the upper floor of the wing was reached. Into this corridor some dozen rooms opened. Here Ella halted for a moment, and held the candle aloft.

"You shall see for yourselves that it could not be any of these doors you heard. We will examine them one by one."

One after another, the doors were tried by Miss Winter. Each door was found to be locked, its key on the outside. When she reached Number Nine, she drew in her breath, and paused for a moment before turning the handle: perhaps she did not like that room more than the girls did. It was the room they had called "her room." But Number Nine was locked as the others were locked, and Ella passed on.

When all the doors had been tried, Ella turned to the servants.

"You see now that you must have been mistaken," she said, speaking very gravely; but in their own minds neither Martha nor Ann would have admitted anything of the kind.

Ella saw that they were not satisfied. Leading the way back to Number Nine, she turned the key, opened the door, and went in. The two girls ventured no farther than the threshold. The room contained the ordinary adjuncts of a bed-chamber, and of one apparently in use. Across a chair hung a servant's muslin apron, on the chest of drawers lay a servant's cap, a linen collar, and a lavender neck-ribbon. Simple articles all, yet the two housemaids shuddered when their eyes fell on them. In a little vase on the chimney-piece were a few withered flowers--violets and snowdrops. The oval looking-glass on the dressing-table was festooned with muslin, tied with bows of pink ribbon. But Ella, as she held the candle aloft and gazed round the room, saw something to-night that she had never noticed before. The bows of ribbon had been untied, and the muslin drawn across the face of the glass so as completely to cover it.

Ella had been in the room some weeks ago, and she felt sure that the looking-glass was not covered then, It must have been done since; but by whom, and why? That none of the servants would enter the room of their own accord she knew quite well: yet whose fingers, save those of a servant, could have done it? Despite her resolution to be calm, her heart chilled as she asked herself these questions, and her eyes wandered involuntarily to the bed, as though half expecting to see there the dread outlines of a form that was still for ever. The same idea struck the two girls.

"Look at that glass!" cried the one to the other, in a half-whisper. "It is covered up as if there had been a death in the room."

Ella could bear no more. Motioning the servants from the room, she passed out herself and relocked the door. But this time she took the key with her instead of leaving it in the lock.

"You see there is nothing to be afraid of," she said to the girls, as she gave them back the candle at the foot of the stairs. "Do not be so foolish again."

But Ella Winter was herself more perplexed and shaken than she allowed to appear, or would have cared to admit.

CHAPTER VI.

ONE SNOWY NIGHT

One of the last houses that you passed before you began to climb the hill into Nullington was the vicarage; a substantial red-brick building of the Georgian era, standing a little way back from the road in a paved fore-court, access to which was obtained through a quaintly-wrought iron gateway. At the back of the house was a charming terraced-garden, with an extensive view, some prominent features of which were the twisted chimneys of Heron Dyke, and the seven tall poplars that overshadowed the moat. Here dwelt the Rev. Francis Kettle, vicar of Nullington-cum-Easterby, and his daughter Maria. The living was not a very lucrative one, being only of the annual value of six hundred pounds; but the vicar was a man who, if his income had been two thousand a year, would have lived up to the full extent of it. He was fond of choice fruits, and generous wines, and French side-dishes; while indoors he never did anything for himself that a servant could do for him. Out of doors, he would potter about in his garden by the hour together. He was sixty years old, a portly, easy-going, round-voiced man, who read prayers admirably, but whose sermons hardly afforded an equal amount of satisfaction to the more critical members of his congregation. To rich and poor alike Mr. Kettle was bland, genial, and courteous. No one ever saw him out of temper. A moment's petulance was all that he would exhibit, even when called from his warm fireside on a winter evening to go through the sloppy streets to pray by the bedside of some poor parishioner. No deserving case ever made a direct appeal to his pocket in vain, although the amount given might be trifling; but he was not a man who, even in his younger and more active days, had been in the habit of seeking out deserving cases for himself. Before all things, Mr. Kettle loved his own ease; ease of body and ease of mind. It was constitutional with him to do so, and he could not help it. He knew that there was much sin and misery in the world, but he preferred not to see them; he chose rather to shut his eyes and walk on the other side of the way. Not seeing the sin and misery, there was no occasion for him to trouble his mind or pain his heart about them. But if, by chance, some heartrending case, some pathetic tale of human wretchedness, did persist in obtruding itself on his notice, and would not be kept out of sight, then would all the vicar's finer feelings be on edge for the remainder of that day. He would be restless and unhappy, and unable to settle down satisfactorily to his ordinary avocations. He would be as much hurt and put out of the way morally, as he would have been hurt physically had he cut his finger. It was very thoughtless of people thus to disturb his equanimity, and cause him such an amount of needless suffering. Next morning, however, the vicar would be his old, genial, easy-going self again, and human sin and wretchedness, and all the dark problems of life, would, so far as he was concerned, have discreetly vanished into the background.

Perhaps it was a fortunate thing for the vicar that he had a daughter--at least, such a daughter as Maria. Whatever shortcomings there might be on the father's part were more than compensated for on the daughter's. Maria Kettle was one of those women who cannot be happy unless they are striving and toiling for someone other than themselves. Her own individuality did not suffice for her: she lost herself in the wants and needs of others. No one knew the little weaknesses of her father's character better than herself, and no one could have striven more earnestly than she strove to cover them up from the eyes of the world. If he did not care to visit among the sick and necessitous of his flock, or to have his easy selfishness disturbed by listening to the story of their troubles, she made such amends as lay in her power. She did more, in fact, being a sympathetic and large-hearted woman, than it would have been possible for the vicar to have done, had his inclinations lain ever so much in that direction. In the back streets of Nullington, and among the alleys and courts where the labouring people herded together, no figure was better known than that of the vicar's daughter, with her homely features, her bright, speaking eyes, her dress of dark serge, her thick shoes, and her reticule. Little children who could scarcely talk were taught to lisp her name in their prayers, and the oldest of old people, as they basked outside their doors in the summer sunshine, blessed her as she passed that way.

Early in the present year, the state of the vicar's health had caused alarm, and he was ordered to the South of France. Maria could not let him go alone, and for the time being the parish had to be abandoned to its fate, and to the ministrations of a temporary clergyman. Maria felt a prevision that she should find most things turned upside down when she got back to it--which proved to be the case. She and her father, the latter in good health, had now returned, and on the day following their arrival, Miss Winter, all eagerness to see them, set off to walk to the vicarage. She and Maria were close and dear friends.

That she should be required to tell all about everything that had happened since their absence, Ella knew; it was only natural.

More especially about that one sad, dark, and most unexplainable event which had taken place at the Hall in February last. She already shrank from the task in anticipation; for, in truth, it had shaken her terribly, and a haunting dread lay ever on her mind.

About midway between Heron Dyke and the vicarage, lying a little back from the road, was a small inn, its sign, a somewhat curious one, "The Leaning Gate." Its landlord, John Keen, had died in it many years ago, since which time it had been kept by his widow, a very respectable and hard-working woman, who made her guests comfortable in a homely way, and who possessed the good-will of all the neighbours around. She had two daughters, Susan and Katherine, who were brought up industriously by the mother, and were both nice-looking, modest, and good girls. Susan was somewhat dull of intellect. Katherine was rather a superior girl in intelligence and manners, and very clever with her needle; she had been the favourite pupil in Miss Kettle's school, and later had helped to teach in it. Maria esteemed her greatly, and about fourteen months prior to the present time, when Miss Winter was wanting a maid, Maria said she could not do better than take Katherine. So Katherine Keen removed to the Hall, greatly to her mother's satisfaction, for she thought it a good opening for the young girl; but not so much to the satisfaction of Susan.

The sisters were greatly attached to one another. Susan especially loved Katherine. It is sometimes noticeable that where the intellect is not bright the feelings are strong; and with an almost unreasonable, passionate tenderness Susan Keen loved her sister. Katherine's removal to Heron Dyke tried her. She could hardly exist without seeing her daily; and she would put her cloak on when the day's work was done--for Susan assisted her mother in the inn--and run up to the Hall to see Katherine. But Katherine and Mrs. Keen both told her she must not do this: her going so frequently might not be liked at the Hall, especially by ill-tempered Aaron Stone and his wife. Thus admonished, Susan put a restraint upon herself, so as not to trouble anybody too often; but many an evening she would steal up at dusk, walk round the Hall, and stand outside watching the windows, hoping to get just one distant glimpse of her beloved Katherine.

The time went on to February in the present year, Katherine giving every satisfaction at Heron Dyke: even old Aaron would now and then afford her a good word. And it should be mentioned that the girl had made no fresh acquaintance, either of man or woman--she was thoroughly well-conducted in every way.

Miss Winter's own sitting-room and her bedroom were in the north wing. She had chosen them there on account of the beautiful view of the sea from the windows. Katherine slept in a room near her. On the evening of the fifteenth of February they were both in the sitting-room at work; Ella was making garments for some poor children in the village and had called Katherine to assist. Katherine had a headache; it got worse; and at nine o'clock Ella told her she had better go to bed. The girl thanked her, lighted her candle and went; Ella, who went at the same time to her own room to get something she wanted, saw her enter her chamber and heard her lock herself in: and from that moment Katherine Keen was never seen, alive or dead. Before the night was over, Ella--as you will hear her tell presently--had occasion to go to Katherine's room; she found the door unlocked, and

Katherine absent, the bed not having been slept in. Her apron, cap, collar, and neck-ribbon lay about, showing that she had begun to undress; but that was all. Of herself there was no trace; there never had been any since that night.

That she had not left the house was a matter of absolute fact, for old Aaron had already locked and bolted all the doors, and there could be no egress from it. In short, it was a strange mystery, and puzzled everyone. Where was she? What could have become of her? The matter caused endless stir and commotion in the neighbourhood. Old Squire Denison, very much troubled at the extraordinary occurrence, instituted all kinds of inquiries, but to no purpose. Every nook and corner in the spacious house was searched again and again. Aaron Stone, cross enough with the girl oftentimes beforehand, seemed troubled with the rest; his wife declared openly, her eyes round with terror, that the girl must have been 'spirited' away. The grandson, Hubert, was in London at the time, and knew absolutely nothing whatever of the occurrence.

But the sister, Susan, had a tale to tell, and it was a curious one. It appeared that that same morning she had met Katherine in the village, doing an errand for Miss Winter. Susan told her that a letter had come from their brother--a young man older than themselves, who had gone some years before to an uncle in Australia--and that she would bring it to the Hall that evening. However, when evening came, snow began to fall, and Mrs. Keen would not let Susan go out in it, for she had a cold. Presently the snow ceased, and Susan, wrapping her cloak about her, started with the letter. As she neared the Hall the clock struck nine--too late for Susan to attempt to call, for after that hour her visits were interdicted. She hovered about a short while, thinking that haply she might see one of the housemaids hastening home from some errand, and could send in the letter by her, or perhaps catch a glimpse of her darling sister at her window. The sky was clear then, the moon shining brilliantly on the snowy ground. As Susan stood there, a light appeared in Katherine's room. She fancied she saw the curtain pulled momentarily aside, but she saw no more. While thus watching, Susan was startled by a cry, or scream of terror; two screams, the last very faint, but following close upon the other. They appeared to come from inside the house, Susan thought from inside the room, and were in her sister's voice-- of that Susan felt an absolute certainty. A little thing served to terrify her. She ran back home as she had never run before, and burst into her mother's kitchen in a pitiable state. Mrs. Keen and two or three people sitting in the inn took it for granted that the cry must have been that of some night-bird, and the terrified girl was got to bed.

With the morning, news was brought to the inn of Katherine's strange disappearance; and, as already said, she had never been heard of from that day. Nothing could shake Susan's belief that it was her sister's screams she had heard; she declared she knew her voice too well to be mistaken. The event had a sad effect upon her mind: at times she seemed almost half-witted. She could not be persuaded but that Katherine was still in the house at Heron Dyke; and as often as she could escape her mother's vigilance, she would steal up in the dark and hover about outside, looking at the windows for Katherine--nay, more than once believing that she saw her appear at one of them.

Such was the occurrence that had served to shake Miss Winter's nerves, and that she was on her way now to the vicarage to be (as she well knew) cross-questioned about.

Mr. Kettle met her with a fatherly kiss, telling her she looked bonnier than ever, and that there was nothing to compare with an English rose-bud. Maria clasped her in her arms. Ella took her bonnet off and sat down with them in the bow-windowed parlour open to the summer breeze, and for some time it was hard to say whether she or Maria had the more questions to ask and answer. Then the vicar began, as a matter of course, about the shortcomings in the parish during his absence, especially about the churchwardens' difficulties with Pennithorne--the temporary parson. That gentleman had persisted in having two big candlesticks on the altar where no such articles had ever been seen before, and had attempted to establish a daily service, which had proved to be an ignominious failure, together with other changes and innovations that were more open to objection. Ella confirmed it all, and the vicar worked himself into a fume.

"Confound the fellow!" he exclaimed, "I'd never have gone away had I known. Who was to suspect that meek-looking young jackanapes, with his gold-rimmed spectacles, had so much mischief in him? He looked as mild as new milk. And now, my dear, what about that strange affair concerning Katherine Keen?" resumed the vicar, after a pause. "Your letter to us, describing it, was hardly--hardly credible."

"I can quite believe that it must have seemed so to you," replied Ella.

"Well, child, just go over it now quietly."

The light died out of Ella's eyes, and her face saddened. But she complied with the request, not dwelling very minutely upon the particulars. The vicar and Maria listened to her in silence.

"It is the most unaccountable thing I ever heard of," cried the vicar, impulsively, when it was over. "Locked up in her room, and disappeared! Is there a trap-door in the floor?"

Ella shook her head.

"The waxed boards of the room are all sound and firm."

"And she could not have come out of her room and got out of the house, you say?"

"No. It was not possible. She had a bad headache, as I tell you, and I told her she had better go to bed; that was about nine o'clock. While she was folding up the child's petticoat she had been sewing at, Aaron came into the room to say that Uncle Gilbert was asking for me. Katherine lighted both the bed candles, which were on a tray outside, and we left the room together. I ran into my own room and caught up my prayer-book, for sometimes my uncle lets me read the evening psalms to him. Katherine was going into her room as I ran out; she wished me goodnight, went in, and locked the door."

"Locked it!" exclaimed the vicar. "A bad habit to sleep with the door locked. Suppose a fire broke out!"

"I used to tell her so, but she said she could not feel safe with it unlocked. She and Susan were once frightened in the night when they were little girls, and had locked their door ever since. I went down to Uncle Gilbert," continued Ella. "Aaron was then bolting and barring the house-door--and, considering that he always carries away the key in his own pocket, you will readily see that poor Katherine had no chance of getting out that way."

"There was the backdoor," said the vicar, who, to use his own words, could not see daylight in this story. "Your great entrance-door is, I know, kept barred and locked always."

"Yes. Aaron went straight to the backdoor from the front, fastened up that, and in like manner carried away the key. Believe me, dear Mr. Kettle, there was no *chance* that Katherine could go out of the house. And why should she wish to do so?"

"Well, go on, child. You found the room empty yourself in the middle of the night--was it not so?"

"Yes--and that was a strange thing, very strange," replied Ella, musingly. "I went to bed as usual, and slept well; but at four o'clock in the morning I was suddenly awakened by hearing, as I thought, Uncle Gilbert calling me. I awoke in a *fright*, you must understand, and I don't know why: I have thought since that I must have had some disagreeable dream, though I did not remember it. I sat up in bed to listen, not really knowing whether Uncle Gilbert had called me, or whether I had only dreamt it----"

"You could not hear your uncle calling all the way up in the north wing, Ella," interrupted Miss Kettle.

"No; and I knew, if he had called, that he must have left his room and come to the stairs. I heard no more, but I was uneasy and felt that I ought to go and see. I put on my slippers and my warm dressing-gown, and lighted my candle; but--you will forgive me my foolishness, I hope--I felt too nervous to go down alone, though again I say I knew not why I should feel so, and I thought I would call Katherine to go with me. I opened her door and entered, not remembering until afterwards that I ought to have found it locked. The first thing I saw was her candle burnt down to the socket, its last sparks were just flickering, and that the bed had not been slept in. Katherine's apron and cap were lying there, but she was gone."

"It is most strange," cried Mr. Kettle.

"It is more than strange," returned Ella, with a half sob.

"And, my dear, had your uncle called you?"

"No. He had had a good night, and was sleeping still."

"Well, I can't make it out. Was Katherine in bad spirits that last evening?"

"Not at all. Her head pained her, but she was merry enough. I remember her laughing early in the evening. She drew aside the curtain by my direction to see what sort of a night it was, and exclaimed that it was snowing. Then she laughed, and said how poor Susan would be disappointed, for her mother would be sure not to let her come up through the snow. Susan was to have brought up a letter they had received from the brother."

"And what is the tale about Susan coming up when the snow was over, and hearing screams? Did you hear them in the house?"

"No; none of us heard anything of the kind."

"But if, as I am told Susan says, it was her sister who screamed in the room, some of you must have heard it."

"I am not so sure of that," replied Ella. "Uncle Gilbert's sitting-room--I had gone down to him then--is very remote from the north wing; and so are the shut-in kitchen apartments. Aaron ought to have heard down in the hall, but he says he did not."

"Then, in point of fact, nobody heard these cries but Susan?"

"Yes; Tom, the coachman's boy, heard them. Tom had been out of doors doing something for his father, and was close to the stables, going in again, when he heard two screams, the last one much fainter than the other. Tom says the cries had a sort of muffled sound, and for that reason he thought they were inside the house. So far, poor Susan's account is borne out."

"And the house-doors were found still fastened in the morning?"

"Bolted and barred and locked as usual, when old Aaron undid them. More snow had fallen in the night, covering the ground well. Katherine has never been heard of in any way since."

Mr. Kettle sat revolving the tale. It was quite beyond his comprehension.

"In point of fact, the girl disappeared," he said presently; "I can make nothing more of it than that."

"That is the precise word for it--disappeared," assented Ella, in a low tone. "And so unaccountably that it seems just as if she had vanished into air. The feeling of discomfort it has left amongst us in Heron Dyke can never be described."

"Do you still sleep in the north wing?" asked Maria, the thought occurring to her. "Oh no. I changed my room after that." Ella had told all she had to tell. But the theme was full of interest, and the vicar and Maria plied her with questions all through luncheon, to which meal they made her stay. She left when it was over; her uncle might want her; and Maria put on her bonnet to walk with her a portion of the way. Their road took them past the "Leaning Gate." Mrs. Keen was having the sign repainted--a swinging gate that hung aloft beside the inn. A girl, the one young servant kept, stood with her arms a-kimbo, looking up at the process. The landlady was a short, active, bustling woman, with a kind, motherly face and pleasant dark eyes.

"How do you do, Mrs. Keen?" called out Maria, as they were passing.

Mrs. Keen came running up, and took the offered hand into both of hers. "I heard you were back, Miss Maria, and glad enough we shall be of it. But--but----"

She could not go on. The remembrance of what had happened overcame her, and she burst into tears.

"Yes, young ladies, I know your kind sympathy, and I hope you'll forgive me," she said, after listening to the few words of consolation they both strove to speak--though, indeed, what consolation could there be for such a case as hers?

"We had been gone away so short a time when it happened!" lamented Maria.

"You left on the first of February, Miss Maria, and this was on the night of the fifteenth," said Mrs. Keen, wiping her eyes with her ample white apron. "Ah, it has been a dreadful thing! It is the uncertainty, the suspense, you see, ladies, that is so bad to bear. Sometimes I think I should be happy if I could only know she was dead and at rest."

"How is Susan?" asked Maria.

"Susan's getting almost silly with it," spoke the landlady, lowering her voice, as she glanced over her shoulder at the house. "She has all sorts of wild fancies in her head, poor girl; thinking--thinking----"

Mrs. Keen glanced at Miss Winter, and broke off. The words she had been about to say were these: "Thinking that Katherine, dead or alive, is still at Heron Dyke."

CHAPTER VII.

COMING TO DINNER

Miss Winter sat in her low chair by the window of her sitting-room in the north wing; for though she had abandoned her bedroom in that quarter, she still, on occasion, sat in that. A closed book lay on her lap, her chin was resting on the palm of one hand, and her eyes, to all appearance, were taking in for the thousandth time the features of the well-known scene before her. But in reality she saw nothing of it: her thoughts were elsewhere. This was Tuesday, the day fixed for Edward Conroy to dine at the Hall. How came it that his image--the image of a man whom she had seen but twice in her life--dwelt so persistently in her thoughts? She was vexed and annoyed with herself to find how often her mind went wandering off in a direction where--or so she thought--it had no right to go. She tried her hardest to keep it under control, to fill it with the occupations that had hitherto sufficed for its quiet contentment, but at the first unguarded moment it was away again, to bask in sunshine, as it were, till caught in the very act, and haled ignominiously back.

"Why must I be for ever thinking about this man?" she asked herself petulantly, as she sat this morning by the window, and a warm flush thrilled her even while the question was on her lips. She was ashamed to remember that even at church on Sunday morning she could not get the face of Edward Conroy out of her thoughts. The good vicar's sermon had been more prosy and commonplace than usual, and do what she might, Ella could not fix her attention on it. She caught herself half a dozen times calling to mind what Conroy had said on Thursday, and wondering what he would say on Tuesday. She had no intention of falling in love, either with him or with any other man; on that point she was firmly resolved. She and Maria Kettle had long ago agreed that they could be of more use in the world, of greater service to the poor, the sick, and the forlorn among their fellow-creatures, as single women than as married ones; and Ella, for her part, had no intention of letting any man carry her heart by storm.

Yet, after making all these brave resolutions, here she was, wondering and hesitating as to which dress she should wear, as she had never wondered or hesitated before; and when the clock struck eleven, she caught herself saying, "In six more hours he will be here." Then she jumped up quickly with a gesture of impatience. She was the slave of thoughts over which she seemed to have no control. It was a slavery that to her proud spirit was intolerable. She could not read this morning. Her piano appealed to her in vain. Her crewel-work seemed the tamest of tame occupations. She put on her hat and scarf, and, calling to Turco, set off at a quick pace across the park. Perhaps the fresh bracing air that blew over the sand-hills would cool the fever of unrest that was in her veins. Once she said to herself, "I wish he had never come to Heron Dyke!" But next moment a proud look came into her face, and she said, "Why should I fear him more than any other?"

Ella Winter has hitherto been spoken of as though she were Mr. Denison's niece; she was in reality his grand-niece, being the grand-daughter of an only sister, who had died early in her married life, leaving one son behind her. This son, at the age of twenty-two, married a sister of Mrs. Carlyon, but his wedded life was of brief duration. Captain Winter and his wife both died of fever in the West Indies, leaving behind them Ella, their only child.

Mrs. Carlyon, a widow and childless, would gladly have adopted the orphan niece who came to her under these sad circumstances, but Squire Denison would not hear of such a thing. He had a prior claim to the child, he said, and she must go to him and be brought up under his care. He had no children of his own, and never would have any: Ella was the youngest and last descendant of the elder branch of the family, and Heron Dyke and all that pertained to it should be hers in time to come, provided always that he, Gilbert Denison, should live to see his seventieth birthday. He had loved his sister Lavinia as much as it was in his nature to love anyone; and her son, had he lived, would, in the due course of things, have been his heir. But he was dead, leaving behind him only this one poor little girl. To Gilbert Denison it seemed that Providence had dealt very hardly by him in giving him no male heir to inherit the family honours. He himself would have married years ago had he anticipated such a result.

For six hundred years the property had come down from male heir to male heir, but now at last the line of direct succession would be broken. "If Ella had only been a boy!" he sighed to himself a thousand times: but Ella was that much more pleasing article--except from the heir-at-law point of view-- a beautiful young woman, and nothing could make her anything else.

On the confines of the park, just as she was about to turn out of it, Ella met Captain Lennox, who was coming to call on the Squire. It was the first time Ella had seen him since her return from London, for the Captain had been again from home. He had aristocratic relatives, it was understood, in various parts of the kingdom, and was often away on visits to them for weeks together.

"You are looking better than you were that night at Mrs. Carlyon's," he remarked, as they stood talking.

"Am I?" returned Ella, a rosy blush suffusing her face--for the idea somehow struck her that Mr. Conroy's presence in the neighbourhood might be making her look bright.

"Very much so, I think. Mrs. Carlyon was not quite satisfied with your looks then. By-the-way," added the Captain, after a pause, "has she recovered her jewels, that were lost that night?"

"No. She is quite in despair. I had a letter from her yesterday. You heard of the loss then, Captain Lennox?"

"I heard of it the following day. Ill news travels fast," he added lightly, noting Ella's look of surprise.

"How did you hear of it? I fancied you left London that day."

"No, the next. I heard of it from young Cleeve. He called on Mrs. Carlyon that morning, and came back in time for me and Bootle to see him off. Cleeve told us of the loss on the way to the station. It was a time of losses, Miss Winter. I lost my purse, and poor Bootle his watch--one he valued--the same night."

"Yes, Freddy told us of it later. He thought you were robbed in the street."

"I know he thought so. I did at first. But our losses were nothing compared with Mrs. Carlyon's jewels," continued Captain Lennox rapidly, as though he would cover his last words. "And the jewel-case was found the next day; and the thief must have walked off with the trinkets in his pocket!"

"Just so. And they were worth quite three hundred pounds."

Captain Lennox opened his eyes.

"Three hundred pounds! So much as that! I wonder how they were taken! By some light-handed fellow, I suppose, who contrived to find his way upstairs amid the general bustle of the house."

"No, we think not. The servants say it was hardly possible for anyone to do that unnoticed; Aunt Gertrude thinks the same; And the servants are all trustworthy. It is a curious matter altogether."

Captain Lennox looked at her.

"Surely you cannot suspect any of the guests?"

"It would be uncharitable to do that," was Ella's light answer. But the keen-witted Captain noticed that she did not deny it more emphatically.

"What a pity that the jewels were not safely locked up!" he exclaimed.

"The dressing-room, in which they were, was locked; at least, the key was turned--and who would be likely to intrude into it? Aunt Gertrude remembers that perfectly. She found Philip Cleeve lying on the sofa in her boudoir with a bad headache, and she went into the dressing-room to get her smelling-salts, unlocking the door to enter. Whether she relocked it is another matter."

"Did Cleeve notice whether anybody else went in while he was lying there?"

"He thinks not, but he can't say for certain--we asked him that question the next morning. He fancies that he fell asleep for a few minutes: his head was very bad. Anyway, the jewels are gone, and Aunt Gertrude can get no clue to the thief, so it is hopeless to talk of it," concluded Ella, somewhat wearily. "How is your sister?"

"Quite well, thank you. Why don't you come and see her?"

"I will; I have been very busy since I came home. And tell her, please, that I hope she will come to see me. Good-bye for the present, Captain Lennox: you are going on to my uncle; perhaps you will not be gone when I get back; I shall not be very long."

Ella tripped lightly on, Turco striding gravely beside her. Captain Lennox stood for a minute to look after her.

"I wonder," he muttered to himself, stroking his whiskers--a habit of his when he fell into a brown study--"whether it has crossed Mrs. Carlyon's mind to suspect Philip Cleeve?"

After all her vacillation, Ella went down to dinner that evening in a simple white dress. She could hardly have chosen one to suit her better; at least, so thought Mr. Conroy, when he entered the room. The dinner was not homely, as on the first occasion of his dining there; Ella had ordered it otherwise. It was served on some of the grand old family plate, not often brought to light; and the table was decorated with flowers from the Vicar's charming garden.

But what surprised Aaron more than anything else was to see his master dressed, and wearing a white cravat. He went about the house muttering, *sotto voce*, that there were no fools like old fools, and if these sort of extravagant doings were about to set in at the Hall--soups and fish and foreign kickshaws--it was time old-fashioned attendants went out of it. The Squire, in fact, had so thoroughly inoculated the old man with his own miserly ways, that for Aaron to see an extra shilling spent on what he considered unnecessary waste, was to set him grumbling for a day.

Whether it was that Ella had a secret dread of passing another evening alone with Conroy, or whether her intention was to render the evening more attractive to him, she had, in any case, asked her uncle to allow her to invite the Vicar and Maria, Lady Cleeve and Philip, and Captain Lennox and his sister, to meet Mr. Conroy at dinner. But here the Squire proved obstinate. Not one of the people named would he invite, or indeed anyone else.

"That young artist fellow is welcome to come and take pot-luck with us," he said, "but I'll have none of the rest. And why I asked him, I'm sure I don't know. There was something about him, I suppose, that took my fancy; though what right an invalid man like me has to have fancies, is more that I can tell."

Conroy seemed quite content to find himself the solitary guest. Ella was more reserved and silent than he had hitherto seen her, but he strove to interest her and melt her reserve; and after a time he succeeded in doing so. Once or twice, at first, when she caught herself talking to him with animation, or even questioning him with regard to this or the other, she suddenly subsided into silence, blushing inwardly as she recognised how futile her resolves and intentions had proved themselves to be. Conroy seemed not to notice these abrupt changes, and in a little while Ella would again become interested, again her eyes would sparkle, and eager questions tremble on her lips. Then all at once an inward sting would prick her, her lips would harden into marble firmness and silence. But these alternations of mood could not last for ever, and by-and-by the charm and fascination of the situation proved too much for her. "After this evening I shall probably never see him again," she pleaded to herself, as if arguing with some inward monitor. "What harm can there be if I enjoy these few brief hours?"

Mr. Denison was more than usually silent. Now and then, after dinner, he dozed for a few minutes in his huge leathern chair; and presently, as though he yearned to be alone, he suggested that Conroy and Ella should take a turn in the grounds.

Ella wrapped a fleecy shawl round her white dress, and they set out. Traces of sunset splendour still lingered in the western sky, but from minute to minute the dying colours changed and deepened: saffron flecked with gold fading into sea-green, and that into a succession of soft opaline tints and pearly greys, edged here and there with delicate amber; while in mid-sky the drowsy wings of darkness were creeping slowly down.

They walked on through the dewy twilight glades of the park. Conroy seemed all at once to have lost his speech. Neither of them had much to say, but to both the silence exhaled a subtle sweetness. There are moments when words seem a superfluity--almost on impertinence. To live, to breathe--to feel that beside you is the living, breathing presence of the one supremely loved, is all that you ask for. It is well, perhaps, that such sweetly dangerous moments come so seldom in a lifetime.

They left the park by a wicket, took a winding footway through the plantation beyond, and reached the sand-hills, where they sat down for a few moments. Before them lay the sea, touched in mid-distance with faint broken bars of silvery light; for by this time the moon had risen, and all the vast spaces of the sky were growing brighter with her presence.

"How this scene will dwell in my memory when I am far away!" exclaimed Conroy at length.

"Are you going far away?" asked Ella, in a low voice.

"I received a letter from head-quarters this morning, bidding me hold myself in readiness to start for Africa at a few hours' notice."

"For Africa! That is indeed a long way off. Why should you be required to go to Africa?"

"The King of Ashantee is growing troublesome. We are likely before long to get from words to blows. War may be declared at any moment."

"And the moment war is declared you must be ready to start?"

"Even so. Wherever I am sent, there I must go."

"Yours is a dangerous vocation, Mr. Conroy. You run many risks."

"A few--not many. As for danger, there is just enough of it to make the life a fascinating one."

"Yes; if I were a man I don't think I could settle down into a quiet country gentleman. I should crave for a wider horizon, for a more adventurous life, for change, for----"

She ended abruptly. Once again her enthusiasm was running away with her. There was a moment's silence, and then she went on, laughing:

"But I am content to be as I am, and to leave such wild rovings to you gentlemen! And now we must go back to my uncle, or he will wonder what has become of us."

Little was said during the walk back. Despite herself, Ella's heart sank at the thought of Conroy's going so far away. She asked, mentally and impatiently, what it could matter to her where he went. Had she not said twenty times that tomorrow all this would seem like a dream, and that in all likelihood she and Conroy would never meet again? What matter, then, so long as they did not see each other, whether they were separated by five miles or five thousand?

"Body o' me! I thought you were lost," exclaimed the Squire, as they re-entered the room. "Been for a ramble, eh? seen the sea! Fine evening for it.

And when do you come down into this part of the country again, Mr. Sketcher?"

"That is more than I can say, sir. My movements are most erratic and uncertain."

"Mr. Conroy thinks it not unlikely he may be sent to Africa--to Ashantee," said Ella, a little ring of pathos in her voice.

"Ah--ah--nothing like plenty of change when you are young. Bad climate, though, Ashantee, isn't it? You'll have to be careful Yellow Jack doesn't lay you by the heels. He's a deuce of a fellow out there, from all I've heard. Eh?"

"I must take my chance of that, sir, as other people have to do."

"You talk like a lad of spirit. Snap your fingers in the face of Yellow Jack, and ten to one he'll glance at you and pass you by. It's the tremblers he lays hold of first."

"Why should you be chosen, Mr. Conroy, for these posts of danger?" inquired Ella. "Cannot some one else share such duties?"

"Is it not possible that I may prefer such duties to any other? They do not suit everyone. As it happens they suit me."

"Have you no mother or sister--who may fear your running into unnecessary dangers?"

"I have neither mother nor sister. I have a father; but he lets me do what seems right in my own eyes."

Mr. Denison took what for him was a very cordial leave of Conroy.

"If I am alive when you come back," he said, as he held the younger man's hand in his for a moment, "do not forget that there will be a welcome for you at Heron Dyke. If I am not alive--then it won't matter, so far as I am concerned."

Ella took leave of Conroy at the door. Hardly more than a dozen words passed between them.

"If you must go to Africa," she said, "I hope you will not run any needless risks."

"I will not. I promise it."

"We shall often think of you," she added, in a low voice.

"And I of you, be you very sure."

Her fingers were resting in his hand. He bent and pressed them to his lips, and--the next moment he was gone.

CHAPTER VIII.

AT THE LILACS

Nullington was a sleepy little town, standing a mile, or more, from Heron Dyke, and boasted of some seven or eight thousand inhabitants. The extension of the railway to Nullington was supposed to have made a considerable addition to its liveliness and bustle: but that could only be appreciated by those who remembered a still more sleepy state of affairs, when the nearest railway station was twenty miles away, and when the Mermaid coach seemed one of those institutions which must of necessity last for ever.

Nullington stood inland. Of late years a sort of suburb to the old town had sprung up with mushroom rapidity on the verge of the low sandy cliffs that overlooked the sea, to which the name of New Nullington had been given. Already New Nullington possessed terraces of lodging-houses, built to suit the requirements of visitors, and some good houses were springing up year by year. Several well-to-do families, who liked "the strong sweet air of the North Sea," had taken up their residence there *en permanence.*

It was a pleasant walk from New Nullington along the footpath by the edge of the cliff, with the wheat-fields on one hand and the sea on the other. When you reached the lighthouse, the cliff began to fall away till it became merged in great reaches of shifting sand, which stretched southward as far as the eye could reach. Here, at the junction of cliff and sand, was the lifeboat station, while a few hundred yards inland, and partly sheltered from the colder winds by the sloping shoulder of the cliff, stood the little hamlet of Easterby. A few fishermen's cottages, a few labourers' huts--and they were little better than huts--an alehouse or two, a quaint old church which a congregation of fifty people sufficed to fill, and a few better-class houses scattered here and there, made up the whole of Easterby.

Easterby and New Nullington might be taken as the two points of the base of a triangle, with the sea for their background, of which the old town formed the apex. The distance of the latter was very nearly the same from both places. About half-way between Easterby and the old town of Nullington, you came to the lodge which gave access to the grounds and Hall of Heron Dyke.

On the other side of Nullington, on the London road, stood Homedale, a pretty modern-built villa, standing in its own grounds, the residence of Lady Cleeve and her son Philip.

Lady Cleeve had not married until late in life, and Philip was her only child. She had been the second wife of Sir Gunton Cleeve, a baronet of good family but impoverished means. There was a son by the first marriage, who had inherited the title and such small amount of property as came to him by entail. The present Sir Gunton was in the diplomatic service at one of the foreign courts. He and his step-mother were on very good terms. Now and then he wrote her a cheery little note of a dozen lines, and at odd times there came a little present from him, just a token of remembrance, which was as much as could be expected from so poor a man.

Lady Cleeve had brought her husband fifteen thousand pounds in all, the half of which only was settled on herself; and her present income was but three hundred and fifty pounds a year. The house, however, was her own. She kept two women-servants, and lived of necessity a plain and unostentatious life; saving ever where she could for Philip's sake. That young gentleman, now two-and-twenty years old, was not yet in a position to earn a guinea for himself; though it was needful that he should dress-well and have money to spend, for was he not the second son of Sir Gunton Cleeve?

For the last two years Philip had been in the office of Mr. Tiplady, the one architect of whom Nullington could boast, and who really had an extensive and high-class practice. Mr. Tiplady had known and respected Lady Cleeve for a great number of years; and, being quite cognisant of her limited means, he had agreed to take Philip for a very small premium, but as yet did not pay him any salary. The opening was not an unpromising one, there being some prospect that Philip might one day succeed to the business, for the architect had neither chick nor child.

Another prospect was also in store for Philip--that he should marry Maria Kettle. The Vicar and Lady Cleeve, old and firm friends, had somehow come to a tacit notion upon the point years ago, when the children were playfellows together; and Philip and Maria understood it perfectly--that they were some day to make a match of it. It was not distasteful to either of them. Philip thought himself in love with Maria; perhaps he was so after a fashion; and there could be little doubt that Maria loved Philip with all her heart. And though she could not see her way clear to leave the parish as long as her father was vicar of it, she did admit to herself in a half-conscious way that if, in the far, very far-off future, she could be brought to change her condition, it would be for the sake of Philip Cleeve.

Midway between the old town and the new one, was The Lilacs, the pretty cottage ornée of which Captain Lennox and his sister, Mrs. Ducie, were the present tenants. The cottage was painted a creamy white, and had a verandah covered with trailing plants running round three sides of it. It was shut in from the high-road by a thick privet-hedge and several clumps of tall evergreens. Flower-borders surrounded the house, in which was shown the perfection of ribbon-gardening, and the well-kept lawn was big enough for Badminton or lawn-tennis. There was no view from the cottage beyond its own grounds. It lay rather low, and was perhaps a little too much shut in by trees and greenery: all the same, it was a charming little place.

Here, on a certain evening in September, for the weeks have gone on, a pleasant little party had met to dine. There was the host, Captain Lennox. After him came Lord Camberley, a great magnate of the neighbourhood. The third was our old acquaintance, Mr. Bootle, with his eye-glass and his little fluffy moustache. Last of all came handsome Philip Cleeve, with his brown curly hair and his ever-ready smile. The only lady present was Mrs. Ducie.

Teddy Bootle had run down on a short visit to Nullington, as he often did. He and Philip had found Captain Lennox and Lord Camberley in the billiard-room of the Rose and Crown Hotel--Master Philip being too fond of idling away his hours, and just now it was a very slack time at the office. Lennox at once introduced Mr. Bootle to his lordship, and he condescended to be gracious to the little man, whose income was popularly supposed to be of fabulous extent. Philip he knew to nod to; but the two were not much acquainted. The Captain proposed that they should all go home and dine with him at The Lilacs, and he at once scribbled a note to his sister, Mrs. Ducie, that she might be prepared for their arrival.

Lord Camberley was a good-looking, slim-built, dark-complexioned man of eight-and-twenty. He had a small black moustache, his hair was cropped very short, and he was fond of sport as connected with the racecourse. By his father's death a few months ago he had come into a fortune of nine thousand a year. He lived, when in the country, at Camberley Park, a grand old Elizabethan mansion about five miles from Nullington, where his aunt, the Honourable Mrs. Featherstone, kept house for him.

It was at the billiard-table that he and Lennox had first met. A billiard-table is like a sea voyage: it brings people together for a short time on a sort of common level, and acquaintanceships spring up which under other circumstances would never have had an existence. The advantage is that you can drop them again when the game is over, or the voyage at an end: though people do not always care to do that. In the dull little town of Nullington the occasional society of a man like Captain Lennox seemed to Lord Camberley an acquisition not to be despised. They had many tastes and sympathies in common. The Captain was always well posted up in the state of the odds; in fact, he made a little book of his own on most of the big events of the year. There were few better judges of the points of a horse or a dog than he. Then he could be familiar without being presuming: Lord Camberley, who never forgot that he was a lord, hated people who presumed. Lennox, in fact, was a "deuced nice fellow," as he more than once told his aunt. Meanwhile he cultivated his society a good deal: he could always drop him when he grew tired of him, and it was his lordship's way to grow tired of everybody before long.

Five minutes after they had assembled Margaret Ducie entered the room. Lord Camberley had seen her several times previously, but to Bootle and Philip she was a stranger. Her brother introduced them. There was perhaps a shade more cordiality in the greeting she accorded to Bootle than in the one she vouchsafed to Philip. Camberley, the cynical, who was looking on, and who prided himself, with or without cause, on his knowledge of the sex, muttered under his breath, "She knows already which is the rich man and which the poor clerk. Lennox must have put her up to that."

Mrs. Ducie was a brunette. She had a great quantity of jet-black silky hair, and large black liquid eyes. Her nose was thin, high-bred, and aquiline, and she rarely spoke without smiling. Her figure was tall and somewhat meagre in its outlines; but whether she sat, or stood, or walked, every movement and every pose was instinct with a sort of picturesque and unstudied grace. She dressed very quietly, and when abroad her almost invariable wear was a gown of some plain black material. But about that simple garment there was a style, a fit, a suspicion of something in cut or trimming, in the elaboration of a flounce here or the addition of a furbelow there, that to the observant mind hinted at the latest Parisian audacity, and of secrets which as yet were scarcely whispered beyond Mayfair. The ladies of Nullington and its neighbourhood could only envy and admire, and imitate afar off.

Mrs. Ducie was one of those women whose age it is next to impossible to guess correctly. "She's thirty if she's a day," Lord Camberley had said to himself, within five minutes of his introduction to her. "She can't possibly be more than three-and-twenty," was Philip Cleeve's verdict to-day. The truth, in all probability, lay somewhere between the two.

Whatever her age might be, Lord Camberley had a great admiration for Mrs. Ducie, but it was after a fashion of his own. He was thoroughly artificial himself, and rustic beauty, or simplicity eating bread and butter in a white frock, had no charms for him. He liked a woman who had seen and studied the world of "men and manners;" and that Mrs. Ducie had travelled much, and seen many phases of life, he was beginning by this time to discover. He was on his guard when he first made her acquaintance, lest he might be walking into a matrimonial trap, artfully baited by herself and her brother; for Lord Camberley was a mark for anxious mothers and daughters: not but that he felt himself quite capable of looking after his own interests on that point. Still, however wide-awake a man may believe himself to be, it is always best to be wary in this crafty world; and very wary he was the first three or four times he visited The Lilacs. He was not long, however, in perceiving that, whatever matrimonial designs Margaret Ducie might or might not have elsewhere, she was without any as far as he was concerned; and from that time he felt at ease in the cottage.

Captain Lennox's little dinners were thoroughly French in style and cookery. They were good without being over-elaborate. Camberley's idea was that the pretty widow, despite her white and delicate hands, was oftener in the kitchen than most people imagined. When dinner was over, the gentlemen adjourned to the verandah to smoke their cigars and sip their coffee; while in the drawing-room, the French windows of which were open to the garden lighted only by one shaded lamp, Margaret sat and played in a minor key such softly languishing airs, chiefly from the old masters, as accorded well with the September twilight and the *far niente* feeling induced by a choice dinner.

Philip Cleeve felt like a man who dreams and is yet awake. Never before had he been in the company of a woman like Mrs. Ducie. There was a seductive witchery about her such as he had no previous knowledge of. It was not that she took more notice of him than of anyone else--it maybe that she took less; but he fell under the influence of that subtle magnetism, so difficult to define, and yet so very evil in its effects, which some women exercise over some men, perhaps without any wish or intention on their part of doing so. In the case of Philip it was a sort of mental intoxication, delicious and yet with a hidden pain in it, and with a vague underlying sense of unrest and dissatisfaction for which he was altogether unable to account.

After a time somebody proposed cards--probably it was Camberley--and as no one objected, they all went indoors.

"What are we going to play?--whist?" queried Lennox, while the servant was arranging the table.

"Nothing so slow as whist, I hope," said his lordship. "A quiet hand at 'Nap' would be more to my taste."

"How say you, gentlemen? I suppose we all play that vulgar but fascinating game?" said the Captain.

"I know a little of it," answered Bootle.

"I have only played it once," said Philip.

"If you have played once, it's as good as having played it a thousand times," said Camberley, dogmatically. "I'm not over-brilliant at cards myself, but I picked up Napoleon in ten minutes."

"Shilling points, I suppose?" said Lennox.

Camberley shrugged his shoulders, but said nothing, and they all sat down.

There was an arched recess in the room, fitted with an ottoman. It was Mrs. Ducie's favourite seat. Here she sat now, engaged on some piece of delicate embroidery, looking on, and smiling, and giving utterance to an occasional word or two between the deals, but not interrupting them.

Philip Cleeve, notwithstanding that he was less conversant with the game than his companions, and that the black eyes of Mrs. Ducie would persist in coming between him and his cards--he could see her from where he sat almost without a turn of his head--was very fortunate in the early part of the evening, carrying all before him. He found himself, at the end of an hour and a half's play, a winner of close on three sovereigns, which to a narrow pocket seems a considerable sum.

"This is too sleepy!" cried Camberley at last. "Can't we pile up the agony a bit, eh, Lennox?"

"I'm in your hands," said the Captain.

"What say you, Mr. Bootle?" queried his lordship. "Shall we turn our shillings into half-crowns? That will afford a little more excitement, eh?"

"Then a little more excitement let us have by all means," answered good-natured Freddy, who cared not whether he lost or won.

But now Philip's luck seemed at once to desert him. What with the extra wine he had taken, and the glamour cast over him by the proximity of Mrs. Ducie, his judgment became entirely at fault. In half an hour he had lost back the whole of his winnings; a little later still, his pockets were empty. It is true he only had two sovereigns about him at starting, so that his loss was not a heavy one; but it was quite heavy enough for him. He was hesitating what he should do next--whether borrow of Bootle or Lennox--when all at once he remembered that he had money about him. In the course of the day he had collected an account amounting to twenty pounds, due to Mr. Tiplady, and it was still in his possession. He felt relieved at once. There was a chance of winning back what he had lost. With a hand that shook a little he poured out some wine and water at the side-table, and then sat down to resume his play.

When the clock on the chimney-piece chimed eleven, Lord Camberley threw down his cards, saying he would play no more, and Philip Cleeve found himself with a solitary half-sovereign left in his pocket.

He got up, feeling stunned and giddy, and stepped out through the French window into the verandah. Here he was presently joined by the rest. Lennox thrust a cigar into his hand, and they all lighted up. The night was sultry; but after the warmth of the drawing-room such fresh air as there was seemed welcome to all of them. They went slowly down the main walk of the garden towards the little fish-pond at the end, Camberley and Mrs. Ducie, for she had strolled out too, being a little behind the others.

"I am going to drive my drag to the Agricultural Show at Norwich next Tuesday," said his lordship to her. "Lennox has promised to go. May I hope that you will honour me with your company on the box seat on the occasion?"

"Who is going beside yourself and Ferdinand?" she asked.

"Captain Maudesley, and Pierpoint. Sir John Fenn will probably pack himself inside with his gout."

"But the other ladies--who are they?"

"Um--well, to tell you the truth, I had not thought about asking any other lady."

"Ah! Then, I'm not sure that I should care to go with you, Lord Camberley. Five gentlemen and one lady--that would never do."

"Let me beg of you to reconsider----"

"Pray do nothing of the kind. I would rather not."

"I am awfully sorry," said his lordship, in something of a huff. "Confound this cigar! And confound such old-fashioned prudish notions!" he added to himself. "I'd not have thought it of her."

She walked back, after saying a pleasant word or two, and fell into conversation with Philip Cleeve. He seemed distrait. She thought he had taken enough champagne, and felt rather sorry for the young fellow.

"Do you never feel dull, Mrs. Ducie," he asked, "now that you have come to live among the sand-hills?"

"Oh no. The people I have been introduced to here are all very nice and kind; and then I have my ponies, you know; and there's my music, and my box from Mudie's once a month; so that I have not much time for ennui. My tastes are neither very æsthetic nor very elevated, Mr. Cleeve."

"They are at least agreeable ones," answered Philip.

As Philip Cleeve walked home a war of feelings was at work within him, such as he had never experienced before. On the one hand there was the loss of Mr. Tiplady's twenty pounds; which must be made good tomorrow morning. He turned hot and cold when he thought of what he had done. He knew it was wrong, dishonourable--what you will. How he came to do it he could not tell--just as we all say when the apple's eaten and only the bitter taste left. He must ask his mother to make good the loss; but it would never do to tell her the real facts of the case. He should not like her to think him dishonourable--and she was not well, and it would vex her terribly. He must go to her with some sort of excuse--a poor one would do, so utterly unsuspicious was she. This was humiliation indeed. He was almost ready to take a vow never to touch a card again. Almost; but not quite.

On the other hand, his thoughts would fly off to Margaret Ducie and her thousand nameless witcheries. There was quite a wild fever in his blood when he dwelt on her. It seemed a month since he had last seen and spoken with Maria Kettle--Maria, that sweet, pale abstraction, who seemed to him to-night so unsubstantial and far away. But he did not want to think of her just now. He wanted to forget that he was engaged to her, or as good as engaged. Though some innate voice of conscience whispered that, if he valued his own peace of mind, it would be well for him to keep out of the way of the beautiful ignis fatuus which had shone on his path to-night for the first time.

CHAPTER IX.

THE DOCTOR'S VERDICT

It was just about this time that Squire Denison, dining alone, was taken ill at the dinner-table. Very rarely indeed was Ella out at that hour, but it chanced that she had gone to spend a long evening with Lady Cleeve. The Squire's symptoms looked alarming to Aaron Stone and his wife; and the young man, Hubert, went off on horseback to Nullington, to summon Dr. Spreckley.

The Doctor had practised in Nullington all his life. He was a man of sixty now, with a fine florid complexion; he was said to be a lover of good cheer and to have a weakness for the whisky bottle; though nobody ever saw him the worse for what he had taken. He had a cheerful, hearty way with him, that to many people was better than all his physic, seeming to think that most of the ills of life could be laughed away if his patients would only laugh heartily enough. Mr. Denison had great confidence in him; and no wonder, seeing that he had attended him for twenty years. Dr. Spreckley was not merely the Squire's medical attendant, but news-purveyor-in-general to him as well. Now that the Squire got out so little himself and saw so few visitors at the Hall, he looked to Spreckley to keep him *au courant* with all the gossip anent mutual acquaintances and all the local doings for a dozen miles round; and Spreckley was quite equal to the demands upon him. During the past year or two Mr. Denison had experienced several of the sudden attacks; but none of so violent a nature as was the one this evening. Dr. Spreckley's cheerful face changed when he saw the symptoms, and the look, momentary though it was, was not lost on the sick man.

"Where's Miss Winter?" asked the Doctor, somewhat surprised at her absence.

"Miss Ella's gone to Lady Cleeve's for the evening, sir," answered Mrs. Stone, who was in attendance.

"And a good thing too," put in the Squire, rousing himself. "Look here--I won't have her told I've been ill. Do you hear--all of you? No good to worry the lassie."

Dr. Spreckley administered certain remedies, saw the Squire safely into bed, and stayed with him for a couple of hours afterwards, Aaron supplying him with a small decanter of whisky. The symptoms were already disappearing, and Dr. Spreckley's face was hopeful.

"You'll be all right, Squire, after a good night's rest," said he, with all his hearty cheerfulness. "I'll be over by ten o'clock in the morning."

When Ella returned, as she did at nine o'clock, nothing was told her. "The master felt tired, and so went to bed betimes," was all Mrs. Stone said. And Ella suspected nothing.

While she was breakfasting the next morning--her uncle sometimes took his alone in his room--Aaron came to her, and said the master wanted her. Ella hastened to him.

"Why! are you in bed, uncle dear?" she exclaimed.

"One of my lazy fits--that's all; thought I'd have breakfast before I got up. Why not? Got a mind for a walk this fine morning, dearie?"

"Yes, uncle, if you wish me to go anywhere. It is a beautiful morning."

"So, so! one should get out this fine weather when one can: wish my legs were as young to get over the ground as they used to be. I want you to go to the vicarage, child, and take a letter to Kettle that I've had here these few days. It's about the votes for the Incurables, and it's time it was attended to. Tell him he must see to it for me and fill it up. Mind you are with him before ten o'clock, and then he'll not be gone out."

"Yes, uncle. I will be sure to go."

"And look here, lassie," added the Squire; "if you like to stay the morning with Maria, you can. I shan't want you; I shall be pottering about here half the day."

Having thus got rid of his niece, the coast was clear for Dr. Spreckley. True to his time, the Doctor drove up in his ramshackle old gig.

"You are better this morning; considerably better," he said to his patient after a quiet examination. "That was a nasty attack, and I hope we shan't have any more of them for a long time to come."

"I was worse, Doctor, than even you knew of," said Mr. Denison. "The wind of the grave blew colder on me yesterday evening than it has ever blown before. Another such bout, and out I shall go, like the snuff of a candle. Eh, now, come?"

"We must hope that you won't have another such bout, Squire," was Dr. Spreckley's cheerful answer.

"Is there nothing you can prescribe, or do, Doctor, that will guarantee me against another such attack?" asked Mr. Denison, with almost startling suddenness.

Dr. Spreckley put down the phial he had taken in his hand, and faced his patient.

"I should be a knave, Squire, to say that I could guarantee you against anything. We can only do our best and hope for the best."

Mr. Denison was silent for a few moments, then he began again.

"Look here, Spreckley; you know my age--on the twenty-fourth of next April I shall be seventy years old. You know, too, what interests are at stake, and how much depends upon my living to see that day."

"I am not likely to forget," said the Doctor. "These are matters that we have talked over many a time."

"Do you believe in your heart, Spreckley, that I shall live to see that day--the twenty-fourth of next April?"

The question was put very solemnly, and the sick man craned his long neck forward and stared at the Doctor with wild hungry eyes, as though his salvation depended on the next few words.

The physician's ruddy cheek lost somewhat of its colour as he hesitated. He fidgeted nervously with his feet, he coughed behind his hand, and then he turned and faced his patient. The signs had not been lost on the Squire.

"Really, my dear sir, your question is a most awkward one," said Spreckley, slowly, "and one which I am far from feeling sure that I am in a position to answer with any degree of accuracy."

"Words--words--words!" exclaimed the sick man, turning impatiently on his pillow. "Man alive! you can answer my question if you choose to do so. All I ask is, do you *believe*, do you think in your own secret heart, that I shall live to see the twenty-fourth of April? You can answer me that."

"Are you in earnest in wishing for an answer, Mr. Denison?"

"Most terribly in earnest. I tell you again that another turn like that of last night would finish me. At least, I believe it would. And I might have another attack any day or any hour, eh?"

"You might. But--but," added the Doctor, striving to soften his words, "it might not be so severe, you know."

"There are several things that I want to do before I go hence and am seen no more," spoke the Squire in a low tone. "You would not advise me to delay doing them?"

"I would not advise you, or any man, to delay such matters."

"You do not think in your heart that I shall live to see the twenty-fourth of April--come now, Spreckley!"

The Doctor placed his hand gently on Mr. Denison's wrist, and bent forward.

"If you must have the truth, you must."

"Yes, yes," was the eager, impatient interposition. "The truth--the truth."

"Well, then--these attacks of yours are increasing both in frequency and violence. Each one that comes diminishes your reserve of strength. One more sharp attack might, and probably would, prove fatal to you."

"You must ward it off, Spreckley."

"I don't know how to."

The Squire lifted his hand slightly, and then let it drop on the coverlet again. Was it a gesture of resignation, or of despair? His chin drooped forward on his breast, and there was unbroken silence in the room for some moments.

"Doctor," said Mr. Denison then, and his tones sounded strangely hollow, "I will give you five thousand pounds if you can keep me alive till the twenty-fifth of April. Five thousand, Spreckley!"

"All the money in the world cannot prolong life by a single hour when our time has come," said the surgeon. "You know that as well as I, Mr. Denison. Whatever human skill can do for you shall be done; of that you may rest assured."

"But still you think I can't last out--eh?"

The Doctor took one of his patient's hands and pressed it gently between both of his. "My dear old friend, I think that nothing short of a miracle could prolong your life till then," and there was an unwonted tremor in his voice as he spoke.

Nothing more was said. Dr. Spreckley turned to the door, remarking that he would come up again later in the day.

"There's no necessity," said the Squire, with spirit, as if he took the fiat in dudgeon and did not believe it. "No occasion for you to come at all to-day. I am better; much better. I should not have stayed in bed this morning, only you ordered me."

"Very well, Squire."

Mr. Denison lay back on his pillow and shut his eyes as the door closed on his friend and physician. Aaron Stone, coming into the room a little later, thought his master was asleep, and went out without disturbing him. An hour later Mr. Denison's bell rang loudly and peremptorily. The Squire was sitting up in bed when Aaron entered the room, and the old man marvelled to see him look so much better in so short a time. "An hour since he was like a man half dead, and now he looks as well as he did a year ago," muttered Aaron to himself. There was, indeed, a brightness in his eyes and a faint colour in his cheeks, such as had not been seen there for a long time; and his voice had something of its old sharp and peremptory tone.

"Aaron, what do you think Dr. Spreckley has been telling me this morning?" he suddenly asked.

"I'm a bad hand at guessing, Squire, as you ought to know by this time," was the somewhat ungracious answer.

"He tells me that I shall not live to see the twenty-fourth of next April."

Aaron's rugged face turned as white as it was possible for it to turn; a small tray that he had in his hands fell with a crash to the ground.

"Oh! master, don't say that--don't say that!" he groaned.

"But I must say it: and what's more, I feel it may be true," returned the Squire.

"I can't believe it; and I won't," stammered the old servant: who, whatever his faults of temper might have been, was passionately attached to his master. Aaron had never seriously thought the end was so near. The Squire had had these queer attacks, it was true: but did he not always rally from them and seem as well as ever? Why, look at him now!

"Spreckley must be a fool, sir, to say such a thing as that! Had he been at the whisky bottle?"

"I forced the truth from him," spoke the Squire. "It is always safest to get at the truth, however unpalatable it may be. Eh, now?"

"I'm fairly dazed," said the old man. "But I don't believe it. When you go, master, it will be time for me to go too."

"It's not that I'm afraid to go," said the Squire--"when did a Denison fear to die?--and Heaven knows my life has not been such a pleasant one of late years that I need greatly care to find the end near. It's the property, Aaron-- this old roof-tree and all the broad acres--you know who will come in for them if I don't live to see next April."

The old serving-man's mouth worked convulsively; he tried to speak but could not. Tears streamed down his rugged cheeks. Pretending to busy himself about the fireplace, he kept his back turned to the Squire.

"If it were not for that, I should not care how soon my summons came," continued Mr. Denison; "but it's hard to have the apple snatched from you at the moment of victory. I would give half that I'm possessed of to anyone who would insure my living to the end of next April. Why not?"

"What's Spreckley but an old woman? he don't know," said Aaron. "Why don't you have some of the big doctors down from London, sir? Like enough they could pull you through when Spreckley can't."

The Squire laughed, a little dismally.

"You seem to forget that I had a couple of bigwigs down from London on the same errand some months ago. They and Spreckley had a consultation, and what was the result? They fully endorsed all that he had done, and said that they themselves could not have improved on his method of treatment. It would not be an atom of use, old comrade, to have them down again. That's my belief."

It was not Aaron's. He had no particular opinion of Spreckley--and he was fearfully anxious.

"Poor Ella! Poor lassie!" murmured the Squire, very gently. "I always hoped she would be the mistress of Heron Dyke when I was gone. But--but--but----" He broke off. He could not speak of it. Things just now seemed very bitter, grievously hard to bear.

"Won't you get up, master?"

"Not just now. You can come in by-and-by, Aaron," replied the Squire: and Aaron crept out of the room without another word.

The sitting-room of Aaron Stone and his wife was a homely apartment, opening from the kitchen. To this he betook himself, shut the door behind him, and sat down in silence. Dorothy had her lap full of white paper, cutting it out in fringed rounds to cover some preserves that had been made. Happening to look at her husband, she saw the tears trickling fast down his withered cheeks.

Dorothy's eyes and mouth alike opened. She gazed at him with a mixture of curiosity and alarm. Not for twenty years had she seen such a sight. Pushing back her silver hair under her neat white cap, she dropped the scissors and the paper, and sat staring.

"What is it?" she asked in a faint voice, picturing all kinds of unheard-of evils. "Anything happened to the lad, Aaron?"

"The lad" was Hubert, her grandson. He was very dear to Dorothy: perhaps not less so to Aaron. Aaron did not answer; could not: and, as if to relieve her fears, Hubert came in the next moment.

"Why, grandfather, what on earth has come to you?" cried the young man, no less astonished than Dorothy.

With a half sob, Aaron told what had come to them: the trouble had taken all his crusty ungraciousness out of him. The master was going to die. Spreckley said he could not keep him alive until next April. And Miss Ella would have to turn out of Heron Dyke to make way for those enemies, the other branch. And they should have to turn out too; and he and Dorothy, for all he knew, would die in the workhouse!

An astounding revelation. No one spoke for a little while. Then Dorothy began with her superstitions.

"I knew we should have a death in the house before long. There's been a winding-sheet in the candle twice this week; and on Sunday night as I came over the marshes three corpse-candles appeared there, and seemed to follow me all the way across. I didn't think it would be the Squire, though: I thought of Bolton's wife."

Bolton was the coachman, and his wife was delicate.

"Hush, granny!" reproved Hubert; "all that is nonsense, you know. Why does not the Squire call in further advice?" he added after a pause. "Spreckley's not good for much save a gossip."

"I asked him why not," said Aaron; "but he seems to think his time is come. If they could only keep him alive till next April, he says: that's all he harps upon."

"And I am sure there must be means of doing it," cried Hubert. "What one medical man can't do, another may. I have a great mind to call in Dr. Jago--saying nothing about it beforehand. He is wonderfully clever."

"The master might not forgive you, Hubert."

"But if the new man could prolong his life!" debated Hubert. "I'll think about it," he added, catching up his low-crowned hat.

He walked across the yard in his well-made shooting-coat that a lord might wear, and whistled to one of the dogs. The two housemaids stood in what was called the keeping-room, ironing fine things at the table underneath the window. They looked after the young man with admiring eyes. He held himself aloof from them, as a master does from a servant, but the girls liked him, for in manner to them he was civil and kind.

"Is he not handsome?" cried Ann. "And aren't both the old people proud of him?"

"What do you think I saw last night?" said Martha in a low tone, as Hubert Stone disappeared through the green door leading to the shrubbery. "I was coming home from that errand to Nullington, when, out there in the park, hiding behind a tree and peering at our windows here, was a grey figure that one might have taken for a ghost--poor Susan Keen. She did give me a turn, though."

"I wonder they don't stop her watching the house at night in the way she does," returned Ann, shaking out one of Mrs. Stone's muslin caps. "It gives one a creepy feeling to have her watching the windows like that--and to know what she's watching for."

"You know what she says, Ann!"

"Yes, I know; and a very uncomfortable thing it is," rejoined the younger servant. "If she sees Katherine at the window----"

"She told me again last night that she does see her," interrupted the elder; "has seen her three times now, in all. She says that Katherine stands at the window of her old room, in the moonlight."

Ann began to tremble; she was nearly as superstitious as old Dorothy.

"Don't you see what it implies, Martha? If Katherine is seen at the window, she must be in the house, that's all. I wish they'd have that north wing barred up!"

"You are ironing that net handkerchief all askew, Ann!"

"One has not got one's proper wits, talking of these ghostly things," was Ann's petulant answer, as she lifted the net off the blanket with a fling.

Hubert, meanwhile, was going down to the shore. What he had learnt troubled him in no measured degree, and his busy brain was hard at work. If only this fiat, which threatened evil to all of them, might be averted!

The tide was out, and he walked along the sands, flinging his stick now and again into the water for the dog to fetch out, as he recalled what he had heard about the almost miraculous skill of this Dr. Jago; who was said, nevertheless, to be an unscrupulous man in his remedies--kill or cure. Could he keep that life in Mr. Denison, which, as it appeared, Dr. Spreckley could not? These bold practitioners were often lucky ones. If Jago----

Hubert Stone halted, both in steps and thought. There flashed into his mind, he knew not why, something he had read in an old French work, recently bought: for the young fellow was a good French scholar. It was a case analogous to Mr. Denison's--where a patient had been kept alive, in spite of nature--or almost in spite of it. The means tried then, which were minutely described, might answer now. Hubert's breath quickened as he thought of it. For two hours he slowly paced the sands, revolving this and that.

A strange look of mingled excitement and determination sat on his face when he got back to the Hall. Mrs. Stone lamented to him that the dinner was over, meaning their dinner, and was all cold now. Hubert answered that he did not want dinner; but he wanted to see the Squire if he were alone. Yes, he was alone; and he seemed pretty well now. And not a word was to be breathed to Miss Ella about his illness: these were the strict orders issued.

When Hubert went in he found the Squire seated in his easy-chair in front of the fire. He looked very worn and thin, but his eyes were as resolute and his lips as firmly set as they had ever been.

"After what my grandfather told me this morning I could not help coming to see you, sir," said Hubert. "This is very sad news; but I hope that it is much exaggerated."

"There's no exaggeration about it, boy. You see before you, I fear, a dying man. Come now!"

"I am very, very sorry to hear it."

"Ay--ay--good lad, good lad! Some of you will miss me a bit, eh?"

"We shall all miss you very much, Squire: we shall never have such a master again. Of course, sir, I know that your great wish all along has been to live till your seventieth birthday had come and gone. Surely you will live to see that wish fulfilled!"

"That's just what I shan't live to see, if Spreckley's right," answered the Squire, and his face darkened as he spoke. "For my life I care little; it has been like a flickering candle these few years past. It's the knowledge that the estate will go away, from my pretty birdie, to a man whom I have hated all my life, that tries me. It is like the taste of Dead Sea apples in my mouth."

Hubert drew his chair a little nearer--for he had been bidden to sit.

"If you will pardon me, sir, for saying it, I do not think you ought to take what Dr. Spreckley says for granted. You should have better advice."

"The London doctors have been down once--and they did me no good. They'd not do it now. And there'd be the trouble and expense incurred for nothing."

"I was not thinking of London doctors, sir, but of one nearer home--Dr. Jago."

"Pooh! They say he is a quack."

Hubert Stone bent his head, and talked low and earnestly--describing what he had heard of Dr. Jago's wonderful skill.

"I--I know a little of medicine myself, sir," he added; "sometimes I wish I had been brought up to it, for I believe I have a natural aptitude for the science, and I read medical books, and have been in hospitals; and--and I think, Squire, that a clever practitioner who knows his business could at least keep you alive until next April. Ay, and past it. I almost think *I* could."

Mr. Denison smiled. The idea of Hubert dabbling in such things tickled him.

"Well, and how would you set about it?" he demanded in pleasant mockery.

Hubert said a few words in a low tone; his voice seemed to grow lower as he continued. He looked strangely in earnest; his face was dark and eager.

"The lad must be mad--to think he could keep me alive by those means!" interrupted the Squire, staring at Hubert from under his shaggy brows, as though he half thought he saw a lunatic before him.

"If you would only let me finish, sir--only listen while I describe the treatment----"

"Pray, did you ever witness the treatment you would describe--and see a life prolonged by it?"

Without directly answering the question, Hubert resumed the argument in his low and eager tones. Gradually the Squire grew interested--perhaps almost unto belief.

"And you could--could doctor me up in this manner, you think!" he exclaimed, lifting his hand and letting it drop again. "Boy, you almost take my breath away."

"Perhaps I could not, sir. But I say Dr. Jago might."

Squire Denison sat thinking, his head bent down.

"Do you know this Dr. Jago?" he presently asked. "Have you met him?"

"Once or twice, sir. And I was struck with an impression of his inward power."

"Well, I--I will see him," decided the Squire. "And if he thinks he can--can keep life in me, I will make it worth his while. Why, lad, I'd give half my fortune, nearly, to be able to will away Heron Dyke out of the clutches of those harpies, who look to inherit it, and who have kept their spies about us here. You may bring this new doctor to me."

A glad light came into Hubert's face: he was at least as anxious as his master that Heron Dyke should not pass to strangers.

"Shall I bring him tomorrow, sir?"

"Ay, tomorrow. Why not? Spreckley will be here at ten; let the other come at noon. But look you here, lad: not a word to him beforehand about this idea of yours, this new--new treatment. I'll see him first."

The clock was striking twelve the following day when Dr. Jago rang at the door of the Hall. He was a little, dark-featured, foreign-looking man of thirty, with a black moustache and a pointed beard, and small restless eyes that seemed never to look stedfastly at anything or anybody, imparting an impression of being always on his guard. He had come to Nullington about a year ago, a stranger to everyone in it, and had started there in practice. His charges were low, and his patients chiefly those who could not afford to pay much in the shape of doctors' bills. But Dr. Spreckley was an elderly man, and Dr. Downes might be considered an old man, so there was no knowing what might happen in the course of a few years. Meanwhile Theophilus Jago possessed his soul in patience, and made ends meet as best he could. It was a great event in his life to be sent for by the Master of Heron Dyke.

"You are Dr. Jago, I think?" began the Squire, who was again in bed; and the Doctor bowed assent.

"I and my medical attendant, Dr. Spreckley, have had a slight difference of opinion. In all probability he will not visit me again, and I have sent for you in the hope that we may get on better together than Spreckley and I did."

"I am flattered by your preference, sir. You may rely upon my doing my best to serve you in every way."

"Probably you may have heard that I have been ill for a long time--people will talk--and, as a medical man, you most likely are aware of the nature of my complaint?"

Dr. Jago admitted this.

"I had a bad attack two days ago. Yesterday I asked Spreckley whether I should last over the twenty-fourth of next April. He told me that I could do so only by a miracle. He says I can't live, and I say that I must and will live over the date in question."

"And you have sent for me to--to----?"

"To keep me alive. Spreckley can't do it. You must. Now, don't say another word till you have examined me."

Not another word did Dr. Jago utter for a quarter of an hour, beyond asking certain questions in connection with the malady. This over, he sat down by the bedside and drew a long breath.

"Well, what's the verdict? Out with it," added the Squire grimly, the old hungry, wistful look rising in his eyes.

"I suppose you want to hear the truth and nothing but the truth, Mr. Denison?" said Dr. Jago.

"That is precisely what I do want to hear. Why not?"

"Then, sir, I think it most probable that Dr. Spreckley is correct. I fear I can only confirm his opinion."

There was a moment or two of silence.

"Then you say, with him, that I shall not live to see the twenty-fourth of April?"

"There is, of course, a possibility that you may do so," replied Dr. Jago, "but the probabilities are all the other way. I am very sorry, sir, to have to tell you this."

"Keep your sorrow until you are asked for it," returned the Squire, drily. "Perhaps you will pour me out half a glass of that Madeira. I am not so strong as I should like to be."

Dr. Jago did as he was requested, and then sat down and waited. Turning on him with startling suddenness, the sick man seized him by the wrist with a grip of iron, to pull him closer, and spoke with a grim earnestness.

"Look here, Jago, it's not of any use your telling me, or a thousand other doctors, that I shall not live to see April. I must and will live till then, and you must see that I do: you must keep me in life. Man! you stare as if I were asking you to kill me, instead of to cure me."

Dr. Jago tried to smile. He evidently doubted whether he had to deal with a lunatic.

"Pardon me, Mr. Denison," he said, "but in your condition you must avoid excitement. Perfect quiet is your greatest safeguard."

The sick man shrugged his shoulders.

"Well, well, you are perhaps right. You know my young secretary--Hubert Stone?"

"A little."

"And I dare say you think him a shrewd, clever young fellow, eh! But he is more clever than you think for, and has dabbled in many a curious science; medicine for one. He--listen, Mr. Physician--he has suggested a mode of treatment by which he believes I may be kept alive. Come now."

Dr. Jago's face expressed a mixture of surprise and incredulity not unmingled with sarcasm. Mr. Hubert Stone would indeed be a very clever gentleman if he could keep life in a dying man.

"*I* do not know of any such treatment, Mr. Denison."

"Possibly not. But I suppose you are open to learn it?"

"If it can be taught me."

"Well, you go into the next room. Hubert is there, I believe, and will explain it to you better than I can. I never bothered my head about physics. When the conference is over come back to me."

Half an hour had elapsed--quite that--and the Squire was growing impatient, when Dr. Jago returned. He was looking, very grave.

"Will the treatment answer?" he cried out impatiently, before the Doctor could speak.

"It might answer, Mr. Denison; I do not say it would not. But--it is dangerous."

"And what if it is dangerous? I am willing to risk it--and I shall pay you well. What! you hesitate? Why, I have heard say that dangerous remedies are not unknown to you; that with you it is sometimes kill or cure."

"In a desperate case possibly. Not otherwise."

"And have you not just told me mine is desperate?"

"True."

"Then you will take me in hand. Bodikins!--if I were telling you to give me a dose of prussic acid as you stand there, you could but look as you are looking. See here. Listen. I will have these--these remedies tried, young man, and by you. I know your skill. I will give you five hundred pounds at once; and I will make it up to two thousand if you carry me over to the twenty-fifth of April."

"I accept the terms," said Dr. Jago, awaking from a reverie, and speaking with prompt decision now his mind was made up. To a struggling practitioner the money looked like a mine of gold: and perhaps Squire Denison's imperative will influenced his. "And I hope and trust I *shall* be able to carry you over the necessary period," he added with intense earnestness. "My best endeavours shall be devoted to it."

Outside the door Hubert Stone was waiting, anxiety in his eyes.

"Yes, I have consented," said Dr. Jago, in answer to their silent questioning. "If we succeed--well. But I cannot forget the risk. And these hazardous risks, if they be discovered, are fatal to the reputation of a professional man."

"Take the book home with you, and study the case well," said Hubert, putting a volume, in the Doctor's hand. "Some little risk there must of course be, but I think not much. It succeeded there: why should it not succeed with Squire Denison?"

That evening Dr. Spreckley received a letter, written by Hubert Stone in his master's name, dismissing him from further attendance at Heron Dyke. The Squire added a kind message and enclosed a cheque; but he very unmistakably hinted that Dr. Spreckley was not expected to call again, even as a friend. Two doctors who held opposing views, and who pursued totally opposite modes of treatment, had better not come into contact with each other.

CHAPTER X.

A DAY WITH PHILIP CLEEVE

When Philip Cleeve opened his eyes the morning after his visit to The Lilacs it took him a minute or two to collect his thoughts, and call to mind all that had happened during the previous evening. In the cold unsympathetic light of early morn his overheated fancies of the preceding night seemed to have little more substance in them than a dream. He could not quite forget Margaret Ducie's liquid black eyes, or the fascination of her smile; but the glamour was gone, and he thought of them as of something that could never trouble his peace of mind again. "It was that champagne," thought Philip. "I had more of it than was good for me."

There was, however, one very tangible fact connected with the doings of the preceding night which would not allow itself to be forgotten. He had gambled away Mr. Tiplady's twenty pounds, and it would have to be his disagreeable duty this morning to ask his mother to make good the loss. Mentally and bodily he felt out of sorts, and out of humour with himself and the world. Very little breakfast did he eat. Lady Cleeve only came down when it was getting time for him to set out for the office. She asked a little about his visit of the previous evening, and also after Freddy Bootle, who was rather a favourite of hers.

"Bootle has promised to dine here tomorrow," said Philip. "This evening I dine with him at the Rose and Crown." He left his seat and went to the window. The disagreeable moment could be put off no longer. Going behind Lady Cleeve's chair, he leaned over and kissed her. "Mother, I am going to ask you to do a most preposterous thing," he said.

"Not many times in your life, dear, have you done that," she answered. "But what is it?"

"I want you to give me twenty-five pounds."

"Twenty-five pounds is a large sum, Philip--that is, a large sum for me. But I suppose you would not ask me for it unless you really need it."

"Certainly not, mother. I need it for a very special purpose indeed."

"Can you tell me for what?"

"No," said Philip, in a low tone. "It--it is for some one," he rather lamely added.

"You are going to lend it! Well, Philip, if it is for some worthy friend who is in want, I will say nothing," said Lady Cleeve, who had implicit confidence in her son. "You shall have the money."

Philip's face was burning. He turned to the window again.

"Do you know that next Tuesday will be your birthday, Philip?" asked his mother. "You will be twenty-two. How the years fly as we grow old! Your asking for this money brings to my mind something which I did not intend to mention to you till your birthday was actually here; but, there is no reason why I should not tell you now. Can you guess, my dear boy, what amount I have saved up, and safely put away for you in Nullington Bank? But how should it be possible for you to guess?"--Philip had turned by this time, and was staring at his mother.

"I have saved up twelve hundred pounds," continued Lady Cleeve. "Yes, Philip, twelve hundred pounds; and on the day you are twenty-two the amount in full will be transferred into your name, and will become your sole property."

"Mother!" was all that the young man could say in that first moment of surprise. Then he took her hand and kissed it.

She smiled, and stroked his curls fondly.

"I need hardly tell you, Philip, that the hope I have had, all along, was that my savings might ultimately be of use in advancing your interests in whatever profession you might finally choose. You have now been two years with Mr. Tiplady, and I gather that you are quite satisfied to remain with him. I have had a little quiet chat with Mr. Tiplady: you know that he and I are very old friends. I named to him the amount I had lying by me in the bank, and hinted to him that he might do worse than take you into partnership. His reply was that he had never hitherto thought about a partner, but that the idea was worth consideration, more especially as he had some thought of retiring from business in the course of a few years. There the matter was left, and I have had no talk with him since, but I think the opening would be a most excellent one for you."

"Twelve hundred pounds seems a lot of money to hand over to old Tiplady," said Philip, with rather a long face.

"Why 'old' Tiplady, dear? He is younger than I am," said Lady Cleeve, with a faint smile. "His business is excellent and superior, as you know; one in which, if you join him, you may rise to eminence. Mr. Tiplady seemed to doubt whether twelve hundred pounds was a sufficient sum to induce him to take you into partnership. And of course it seems ridiculously small compared with the advantages. But I suppose he thinks your connections would go for something--and he is too well off for money to be an object with him. At first you would take but a small share."

Philip shrugged his shoulders and whistled under his breath.

"We can talk of that another time," he said. "How can I thank you enough, mother mine, for this wonderful gift? You are a veritable fairy queen."

In truth, he could not think where so much money had come from. Twelve hundred pounds! He knew the extent of his mother's income and what proportion of it, of late years, had found its way into his own pocket; but he did not know that his mother, in view of some such contingency as the present one, had begun to save and pinch and put away a few pounds now and again even before her husband's death--many years before. The magic of compound interest had done the rest.

Philip Cleeve carried a light heart with him that morning as he set out for the office, and the twenty-five pounds given him by his mother. He had not only got out of his present difficulty easily and without trouble, but in a few short days he would be a capitalist on his own account; he would be one of those favoured mortals, a man with a balance at his banker's, and a cheque-book of his own in his pocket. He could hardly believe in the reality of his good fortune. As for handing over *in toto* to Mr. Tiplady the sum that was coming thus unexpectedly into his possession--it was a matter that required consideration, very grave consideration indeed. But he would have plenty of time to think about that afterwards.

As he crossed the market-place, he stopped to look in the window of Thompson, the jeweller. There was a gold hunting-watch lying in it that he had often admired. In a few days, should he be so minded, he might make it his own. And that pretty signet ring. The price of it was only five guineas, a mere bagatelle to a man with twelve hundred pounds. Hitherto he had never worn a ring, but other young men wore such things, and there was no reason now why he should not do the same. A minute or two later he passed his tailor.

"Good-morning, Dobson," he said with a smile. "I shall look you up in a day or two."

Having to pass the Rose and Crown Hotel on his way to the office, he thought he might as well look up Freddy Bootle. But that gentleman was not yet downstairs, so Philip set out again. As he passed Welland's, the florist, he saw two magnificent bouquets in the window. All at once it struck him that it would not be amiss to pay a morning call at The Lilacs and present Mrs. Ducie with one of the bouquets. Without pausing to reflect, he entered the shop. He was waited on by pretty Mary Welland, the florist's lame daughter, by whose deft fingers the flowers had been arranged. After a little smiling chat, he and Mary being old acquaintances, he chose one of the bouquets and had it wrapped up in tissue paper. The price was half a guinea, but to Philip, in the mood in which he then was, half a guinea seemed a matter of little moment.

Philip had started on his way again, when he encountered Maria Kettle. They both started as their eyes met, and a guilty flush mounted to Philip's brow. Maria at once held out her hand, and her glance fell on the bouquet in its envelope of tissue paper. All in a moment it flashed into Philip's mind that to-day was Maria's birthday. There was little more than the difference of a week between their ages.

"Good-morning, Philip," began Maria. "Papa and I have been wondering what had become of you. You have only been to see us once since we got back."

"The fact is," said Philip in a hesitating way, very unusual with him, "I have been much engaged--Bootle is here now, too, and he has taken up a good deal of my time. But I have not forgotten that this is your birthday, Maria, and----" here he paused and looked at the bouquet. "In fact, I was on my way to----" then he hesitated again and held out the bouquet.

"You were on your way to the vicarage," said Maria, with a smile, "and these pretty flowers are for me. I know they are pretty before I look at them. It was indeed kind of you to remember my birthday."

Philip felt immensely relieved.

"Accept them with my love, Maria," he whispered, and at that moment he felt that he loved her very dearly. Then he pressed one of her hands in his, and spoke the good wishes customary on such occasions. A bright, glad look came into Maria's eyes, and her pale cheek flushed at Philip's words. He turned and walked a little way with her, and then they parted.

Philip sighed as he turned away. What an air of quiet goodness there was about Maria! How sweet and saintly she looked in her dress of homely blue, with the sunlight shining on her!

"If she had lived five hundred years ago, her face would have been painted as that of some mediæval saint," muttered Philip to himself. "She is far away too good to be the wife of such a shuffling, weak-minded fellow as I am."

When he reached the florist's shop on his way back to the office, the remaining bouquet was still in the window. He hesitated a moment, and then went in.

"I will take that other bouquet, if you please, Miss Welland," he said: but Mary noticed that there was no smile on his face this time, as she tied up the flowers. Philip set off in the direction of The Lilacs. He was dissatisfied with himself for what he had done, there was a sore feeling at work within him, and yet his steps seemed drawn irresistibly towards the roof that sheltered Margaret Ducie.

He had got half-way to the cottage when he was overtaken by Captain Lennox in his dog-cart.

"'Morning, Cleeve," called out the Captain; "where are you off to in such a hurry?"

"I didn't know that I was in a hurry," said Philip as he faced round, while that wretched tell-tale flush, which he could not succeed in keeping down, mounted to his face. "The fact is, I was on my way to the cottage," he added. "I thought that I might venture to call on Mrs. Ducie and ask her acceptance of a few flowers."

"And she will be very pleased to see you, I do not doubt," answered Lennox. "I am on the way home myself; so jump up and I will give you a lift."

When they reached the cottage they found Mrs. Ducie practising some songs which she had just received from London. She wore a dress of some soft, creamy material embroidered with flowers, with ornamental silver pins in her hair and a silver snake round one of her wrists. She accepted Philip's flowers very graciously.

"How charmingly they are arranged," she said; "and with what an eye for artistic effect. I must try to paint them before they begin to fade."

Philip begged that he might not interrupt her singing; so she resumed her seat at the piano, and he stationed himself behind her and turned over the leaves of her music. Now that he was here and in her presence, and so near to her that he could have stooped and touched her hair with his lips, the infatuation of last night crept over him again with irresistible force. He was like a man bewitched, from whom all power of volition seems stolen away. She looked even more beautiful this morning in the soft cool twilight of the drawing-room than when seen by lamplight yesterday evening. Nowhere had he seen a woman like her, or one who exercised over him such a nameless but all-powerful charm. By-and-by she persuaded him to sing too.

At last Philip remembered that he must go. The office was not pressed for work just now, and Mr. Tiplady had given him a partial holiday during Bootle's stay: but Philip felt that there was reason in all things. Moreover, Tiplady was away himself to-day.

"When the cat's away," laughed Captain Lennox, upon Philip's saying this.

"I can drive you into the town if you like, Mr. Cleeve," said Mrs. Ducie, who had just reappeared, dressed for going out. "My ponies are at the gate."

Philip accepted the offer gladly.

"I shall see you later in the day," were Lennox's last words to him as he was driven away.

Mrs. Ducie was an accomplished whip, and had a thorough mastery over her high-spirited ponies. Very few minutes sufficed to bring the party to Nullington. They had slackened their pace a little while a load of timber drew out of the way, when Maria Kettle stepped out of a chemist's shop just as they were passing the door. She saw Mrs. Ducie and Philip, and at the same moment they recognised her. A look that was partly surprise and partly trouble came into her eyes; but she bowed gravely and passed on. Mrs. Ducie smiled and bowed; Philip, colouring furiously, greeted Maria with an awkward nod, and then turned away his head. How thoroughly ashamed of himself he felt!

"What a charming young lady Miss Kettle is," said Mrs. Ducie, a minute later.

Philip gave a keen look at his companion's face, but there was nothing to be read there.

"I was not aware that you knew Miss Kettle," he said a little stiffly.

"I have had the pleasure of meeting her three or four times since her return, and Ferdinand and I attend church regularly. I never met anyone who with so much goodness was so entirely unaffected."

It was like heaping coals of fire on Philip's head for him to have to listen to these words. Nothing more was said till the carriage drew up for Philip to alight. Mrs. Ducie held out her hand.

"I hope we shall see you at the cottage again soon, Mr. Cleeve," she graciously said. "I assure you that both to my brother and myself your visits will always be a pleasure."

Philip replied suitably, and went his way. He was grievously annoyed at having been seen by Maria Kettle in the act of driving out with Mrs. Ducie; yet he could not forget how charming the latter was, and how kindly she had received his flowers.

Scarcely had he at length entered the office when Freddy Bootle came in, asking him to take holiday for the rest of the day. The old clerk, Mr. Best, manager in Mr. Tiplady's absence, was agreeable to it. Philip was a favourite of his, and there was not much doing.

Away went Philip and his friend gaily, arm-in-arm. Philip's heels were always light where pleasure was concerned. After eating some luncheon at the Rose and Crown, they adjourned to the billiard-room. Only then did it occur to Philip that the bank-notes his mother had given him in the morning were in his pocket still. He ought to have handed them over to Mr. Best: he had meant to do so, but other matters had put it out of his head.

Lord Camberley and Captain Lennox came in to dinner, in answer to the invitation of Mr. Bootle. Afterwards they all sat talking, over their coffee and cigars. Captain Lennox, the thought striking him, inquired of Bootle whether his lost watch had turned up.

"Not it," said Freddy. "It will never turn up, any more than your purse will. It was an odd thing, when one comes to think of it, that Mrs. Carlyon should have been robbed on the same night. Just as if the same thief had done it all!"

Lord Camberley pricked up his ears.

"How was it?" he asked. "What were the robberies?" And Mr. Bootle related them.

"Pretty good cheek--to leave the case under the curtains and walk off with the baubles!" observed his lordship. "I suppose it was too big to carry away?"

"Too big to carry away unobserved, and too big to be stowed away in a coat, I take it," said Captain Lennox. "How large was it, Cleeve?--you saw it, I think. The fellow must have disposed of the articles about his pockets."

"How large?" repeated Philip, who was sitting with his chair tilted and his head thrown back, puffing forth volumes of smoke in silence, "oh--about *that* large"--making a movement with his hand. "Just give me my coffee-cup, will you, Freddy?"

Later, the party sat down to cards. They began by playing Napoleon, as on the previous evening; but this was changed for the still more dangerous game of Unlimited Loo. At neither one game nor the other was Philip Cleeve anything like a match for those experienced players, Camberley and Lennox, and he grew nervous and excitable. When the party broke up Philip had not only lost the twenty-five pounds given him in the morning by his mother, but fifteen pounds more, for which Lord Camberley held his IOU. As for Freddy Bootle, he did not much care for cards, and he played with a severe indifference to either the smiles or frowns of fortune: if he lost, it was a matter of little consequence to him; if he won, it was a few sovereigns more in the pocket of a man who had already more money than he knew what to do with.

Philip rose from the table with haggard eyes, flushed face, and trembling hands.

"I will redeem my scrap of paper in the morning," he remarked to his lordship.

"All right, old man: you will find me in the billiard-room about four o'clock," answered Camberley. "Only look here, there's no need to be in such a desperate hurry, you know."

He had a dim suspicion that Philip was not over well-off in money matters.

"I shall be in the billiard-room at four," retorted Philip with some hauteur.

He resented the implication in Camberley's words--that perhaps it might not be convenient to pay the fifteen pounds so quickly. His poverty was a matter that concerned no one but himself.

As he walked home alone under the cold light of the stars, and went back in memory to the events of this evening and the last, they seemed to him nothing more than a wretched phantasmagoria, in which only the ghost of his real self had played a part. He was a loser to the extent of forty pounds. And where was he to raise the twenty-five pounds for Tiplady, or the fifteen for Camberley?

There was only one way--by applying to his friend Bootle. It was a disagreeable necessity, but Philip saw no help for it. Bootle was rich and generous, and would lend him the money in a moment. It would only be needed for a few days. The very first cheque he drew, after coming into that twelve hundred pounds, should be one to repay Freddy.

And, thus easily settling his difficulties, Mr. Philip finished up by vowing to himself that he would never touch a card again.

CHAPTER XI.

A VISIT FROM MRS. CARLYON

Dr. Spreckley felt like an angry man. When he read Squire Denison's curt note--curt as to the part of his dismissal--his first impulse was to go up to the Hall and demand an explanation from his old friend and patient. He had been forced into a corner as it were, had been driven into telling a certain disagreeable truth, and now he was discarded for having done so, and a young practitioner of less experience and no note, was taken on in his place! It was very unjust. But Dr. Spreckley never did anything in a hurry. He put the Squire's note away, saying, "I'll sleep upon it."

On the morrow he found that Dr. Jago was really in attendance on the Squire. Dr. Spreckley met him on his way thither in a hired one-horse fly, and received a gracious wave of the hand by way of greeting. "I'll not interfere," exploded the old Doctor in the bitterness of his heart; "I'll never darken Denison's doors again. Unless he sends for me," he added a minute later. "And for all the good *he* can do him"--with a contemptuous glance after Jago--"that won't be long first."

Meanwhile, at the Hall, the Squire was soothing and explaining the change to Ella, who regarded it with dismay.

"I don't like Dr. Jago, Uncle Gilbert. And Dr. Spreckley was our friend of many years."

"And why don't you like Dr. Jago, lassie?"

"I don't know. There's something about him that repels me; it lies in his eyes, I think. I never spoke to him but once."

"When you know more of him, you will like him better," returned the Squire. "I am not sure that *I* like him much, personally. But if he cures me--what shall you say then? Come now!"

"I would say then that I should like him for ever," replied Ella, laughing.

"Well, child, he is hoping to do it. And I think he will."

"Is this true, Uncle Gilbert?"

The Squire patted her cheek.

"What a disbelieving little girl it is! Jago is a wonderfully clever man, Ella; there's no doubt of that: he has studied in foreign schools, and he is about to try an entirely new kind of treatment upon me. He thinks it will turn up trumps, and so do I!"

Ella drew a long, relieved breath.

"Oh, I am so glad, dear uncle! I will make him welcome whenever he comes."

"It is a month to-day since I was outside the house," went on the Squire. "Jago tells me that he shall get me out again in three or four days. The man is a man of power; I see it--I feel it. Give him opportunity, and he will make a great name for himself. We will go about again as we used to, Ella; you and I. Why not?"

Ella's heart leaped; she believed the good news. Her uncle had seemed very poorly indeed lately, but she did not suspect he had any incurable malady, or that he was in any danger.

Dr. Jago came to Heron Dyke day after day. In a short while the Squire was walking about the grounds, leaning on Ella's arm or on Hubert Stone's; and he would be seen again driving through Nullington, his niece seated by his side. Ella had grown to think kindly of Dr. Jago; but that old vague feeling of dislike or distrust she could not quite get rid of. "There is a look in his eyes I never saw in the eyes of anyone else," she said to herself. "He interests me, and yet repels me."

"The Squire will last out yet to will away his property; ay, and longer than that," cried the gossips of the neighbourhood, as they watched the improvement in him. "It will take more than two doctors to kill a Denzon."

And thus October came in. About the middle of that month the Squire sent an invitation to Mrs. Carlyon. It was partly in answer to a letter received from her--in which she told them that a certain projected plan of hers, that of going abroad for the winter, was still in abeyance, for she did not much like the idea of going alone. Higson would attend her of course; but who was Higson?--what she needed was a friend.

"She shall take you, Ella," said the Squire, after the letter of invitation was despatched.

"Take me, uncle! Oh dear, no!"

"And why not, pray, when I say yes?"

"I could not leave you, Uncle Gilbert."

"Oh, indeed! Could you not, lassie?"

"Suppose you were to be taken ill--and I ever so many hundred miles away! Oh, uncle dear, how could you think of it!"

"Well, I hope I am not likely now to be taken ill. Jago is doing me a marvellous deal of good. Don't fear that. I should like you to go abroad for the winter, lassie, and if Gertrude Carlyon goes, we--we will see about it."

Mrs. Carlyon arrived in due course. It had previously been arranged that, if she did go abroad, she should come to them for a short visit first. It seemed to her that she saw a great change for the worse in Mr. Denison; but she was discreet enough to keep her thoughts on the matter to herself, and chose rather to congratulate him on looking so well.

"Ay," said he, complacently, "the new doctor understands me."

"And don't you think Dr. Spreckley did?" asked Mrs. Carlyon.

"Not of late. Spreckley could not do for me what this man will do."

On the second day of her visit, when they were alone, the Squire questioned Mrs. Carlyon about her plans for the winter.

"Have you decided on them, Gertrude?" he asked.

"Not quite," she said. "I suppose, though, I shall go abroad, probably to the South of France. This climate tried my chest severely last winter."

"Ay, I remember. Best for you to go out of it for the next few months."

"An old friend of mine, Mrs. Ord, had decided to accompany me, and now circumstances have intervened to prevent it. That is why I hesitate. I don't care to go so far without a companion."

"You shall take Ella. Come now."

Mrs. Carlyon looked up eagerly.

"Take Ella! Are you in earnest?"

"Never more so. Why not? I had meant to make you and London a present of her for the winter: if you go abroad, so much the better. It will be the greater change for her--and she needs change."

"I shall certainly no longer hesitate if I may have Ella," spoke Mrs. Carlyon, gladly. "But--I should probably stay away four or five months."

"If you stay away six months it would be all the better. To tell you the truth, Gertrude," he continued, seeing Mrs. Carlyon look surprised, "I do not intend my pretty one to be here during the dark months, and you must take her out of my hands. She has never been quite the same since that curious affair up yonder"--pointing over his shoulder in the direction of the north wing.

Mrs. Carlyon began to understand.

"You mean--about Katherine Keen?"

"Ay. Since the girl disappeared----"

"What a most extraordinary thing that was!" interrupted Mrs. Carlyon. "Can you in any way account for it, Squire?"

"There's no way at all of accounting for it. Bodikins, no!"

"I meant, have you any private theory of your own--as to what can have become of her?"

"I know no more what could have become of her than *that*," returned the Squire, touching his stick, and then striking it on the ground to enforce emphasis. "It has troubled me above a bit, Gertrude, I can tell you. She was as nice and inoffensive a young girl as could be. Only the day before she disappeared she ran all across the garden to me to put my umbrella up, because a drop or two of rain began to fall. You can't think what a modest, kind, good little thing she was."

"I always thought it," assented Mrs. Carlyon. "And I esteem her mother; she is so hard-working and respectable. What a trial it must have been for her, poor woman! I shall call and see her before I leave."

"Ay. Why not? Well, it is altogether a very mysterious and unpleasant thing to have happened in this old house, and my pretty lassie, I see, does not forget it. She seems to mope, and to get a bit melancholy now and then. I fancy her eyes are not so bright as they used to be; she doesn't talk so much, or sing so much about the house. It's just as if there was always something hanging over her."

"Of course she must have a change," spoke Mrs. Carlyon.

"She was all the better for her visit to London in spring, but she was not long enough away," went on the Squire. "You know how lonely we are here. My health won't allow of my seeing much company, and Ella doesn't seem to care about extending her acquaintances. It will be horribly dull for her here this winter, with nobody in the house but a sick and cantankerous old man. I wish she could get right away out of England for six or eight months. She would come back to us next spring as merry as a blackbird. Why not, now?"

"I need not say how glad I should be to take Ella with me," said Mrs. Carlyon. "But there's one question--would she go?--would she leave you?"

"Odds bodikins!" cried the Squire, angrily, "is the child to set up her will against mine--and yours? It is for her good--and, go she must."

"Do you think you are in a state to be left for a whole winter alone?" debated Mrs. Carlyon, remembering how greatly she at first thought him changed. "Will Ella think it?"

"I! why I am twenty per cent, better than I was a month ago. There's no fear for me. And, if I became ill at any time, couldn't you be telegraphed to? I say that Ella must have a change for her own sake; and what I say I mean. Come now!"

"Yes; it would no doubt be better for her," assented Mrs. Carlyon, slowly: but, Mr. Denison thought, dubiously.

"Look here, Gertrude: for a woman you've got as sharp a share of sense as here and there one," cried he, lowering his tone as he bent forward towards her. "People have set up all kinds of superstitious notions about the affair; the women here hardly dare stir out of their kitchens after dusk. I find a notion prevails that Katherine is still in the house--is seen sometimes at her window at night. Now, as she can't be in the house alive, you--you must see what that means--folks are such fools, the uneducated ones. But, I put it to you, Gertrude--with this absurd nonsense being whispered about the house, whether it is fit the lassie should spend her winter in it? Eh, now, come!"

He glanced keenly for a moment at Mrs. Carlyon, as if to see whether his words impressed her. And they certainly had.

"No, it is not," she assented, speaking firmly, "and I will take her out of it. But--you speak of the young women-servants, I suppose, Gilbert? It is not at all seemly that they should be allowed to say such things. See Katherine at her window! How absurd! What next?"

"And profess to hear weird sounds about the passages, whisperings, and such like," added the Squire, as if he had pleasure in repeating this.

"What is Dorothy Stone about, to allow it?"

"Dorothy is worse than they are: she always was the most superstitious woman I ever knew. Not a step dare she stir about the house now after dark. Old Aaron is in a rare rage with her; threatens to shake her sometimes," added the Squire with a grim smile.

"There *can't* be anything in it, you know, Gilbert."

"I don't know," he answered: and Mrs. Carlyon stared at him. "After the disappearance of Katherine into--into air, as may be said, one may well believe any marvel. Eh, now?" continued the Squire. "At any rate, Gertrude, it seems to me that we may forgive these poor ignorant people who do believe. But, to go back to the question: Heron Dyke is getting an ill name for mystery, see you, and I do not choose that my innocent lassie shall pass the winter in it."

"Quite right; I perceive all now, and I will take her out of it, Gilbert. At least for two or three of the dark months."

"Two or three months won't do," cried the Squire, testily. "It would be of no use. She must not come back until the days are long and bright."

"Well, well, I see how anxious you are for her," said Mrs. Carlyon; who, however, could hardly feel it right to let him be so long alone. "In any case, you would like her to be home before your birthday."

The Squire did not answer. He seemed to be struggling with some inward emotion, and a curious spasm shot across his face. Mrs. Carlyon half rose from her chair, but sat down again.

"Why before my birthday?" said he, at length. "It's no more to me than any other day. I never make a festival of it as some idiots do--as if it was something to rejoice over. She needn't come back for my birthday unless I send for her. I shall be sure to send if I want her."

"If you became worse--or weaker--you would send?"

"Ay, ay--why not? Don't we always want our dear ones with us in sickness? Not but, what with Jago's treatment, I seem to have taken a new lease of life. Look here: I should like the child to see Italy."

"And so she shall. And she will enjoy it, I am sure, provided she can make her mind easy at leaving you. Ella is not like other girls; she is more reasonable," added Mrs. Carlyon. "Look at some flighty young things-- thinking of nothing but of getting married."

"Bodikins! the women are generally keen enough after that, nowadays. Ella never seems to care for the young fellows. Young Hanerly wanted her, came to me about it; but she'd have nothing to say to him. Whomsoever she marries, he will have to change his name to Denison. None but a Denison must inherit Heron Dyke."

The thought occurred to Mrs. Carlyon--and it was on the tip of her tongue to say it--that Ella's husband might not inherit Heron Dyke. If the ailing man before her did not live to his next birthday, it must all pass away from Ella. But she kept silence.

"I suppose you never by any chance hear from your cousin Gilbert?" she presently asked, the train of thought prompting the question.

Mr. Denison's face darkened; a cold, hard look came into his eyes. He turned sharply round and faced his questioner, but she was directly regarding the smouldering logs on the hearth.

"Hear from my cousin Gilbert!" he said in deep harsh tones. "And pray why should I want to hear from him? I would sooner receive a message from-- from the commonest beggar. He would never have the impudence to write to me. Body o' me! Gilbert, forsooth! He has his spies round the place night and day, I know that; watching and waiting for the moment the breath will go out of me. But they will be deceived--they and their master: yes, Gertrude

Carlyon, I tell you that they will be deceived! I am not dead yet, nor likely to die. I shall live to see my seventieth birthday--I know it, I feel it--and not one acre of the old estates shall go to that man!"

He spoke with strange energy. It was evident that the old hatred towards his cousin still burned as fiercely in his heart as it had done forty years before.

"I am afraid that son of his will prove no credit to the name he bears," Mrs. Carlyon remarked after a pause: and the Squire looked up but did not speak. "I am told that some time ago he had a terrible quarrel with his father. They separated in anger, and he has not been home since. He is supposed to have enlisted as a common soldier and gone out to India."

Mr. Denison gave a sort of savage snarl.

"Ay, ay, that's good news--rare news," he said. "I would give that boy a thousand pounds to keep him away from his father if I only knew where he was--two thousand to anyone who could point out his grave. An only son too. Ah, ah! Rare news!"

At that moment Dr. Jago came in. When he saw the Squire's face, he looked anything but pleased.

"Madam," said he to Mrs. Carlyon, "this must not be. If Mr. Denison is to get permanently better, he must be kept free from excitement. It might counteract all the good I am doing him."

Mrs. Carlyon proposed a walk to Ella that lovely October afternoon, after making an inquiry or two in the household about the unpleasant topic touched on by the Squire. The air was mellow and gracious; and they took their way to the sands, seating themselves on the very spot where Ella had once sat with Edward Conroy. Never did she sit there but she thought of him; of what he had said; of his looks and tones. She wondered whether he was in Africa; she wondered when she should hear of him.

It was low water, and where the vanished tide had been was now a tract of firm yellow sand with hardly a pebble in it; excellent to walk upon. Not till the solitude of the shore was about them did Mrs. Carlyon say a word to her companion on the subject that she had to break to her--their journeying together abroad.

Ella was astonished, hurt; perhaps even a little indignant. Could her uncle really wish her to leave him and to go away for so long when he needed companionship and care? Mrs. Carlyon quietly soothed her, persuaded, reassured her; and finally told her that it was *best it should so be.*

Allowing her niece to go in alone, Mrs. Carlyon turned her steps towards the little inn--the Leaning Gate. She had her curiosity about the doings of that past snowy night in February, just as other people had. The conversation with the Squire and with Dorothy Stone only served to whet it, to puzzle her more than ever, if that were possible; and to enhance her sympathy for poor Katherine's family.

Mrs. Keen was waiting upon a customer who had halted at the inn for the day; Susan had taken her work into the garden. Mrs. Carlyon found her there seated on a rustic bench; she was hemming some new chamber towels. It was a large and pretty garden, filled with homely flowers in summer and with useful vegetables. A great bush of Michaelmas daisies was in blossom now, near the end of the bench. Susan sat without a bonnet, and the sunlight fell on her smooth brown hair, so soft and fine, just the same pretty hair that Katherine had: indeed, there had been a great resemblance between the sisters. She looked neat as usual--a small white apron on over her dark gown, a white collar at the neck. When she saw Mrs. Carlyon she got up to make her courtesy, and the tears filled her mournful grey eyes. That lady sat down by her and began to speak in a sympathising tone of the past trouble.

"It is not past, ma'am," said Susan, in answer to a remark; "it never will be."

"My good girl, I wanted to talk to you," said Mrs. Carlyon; "I came on purpose. What I have heard about you grieves me so much----"

But here she stopped, for Mrs. Keen came running from the house to greet the visitor. The landlady was a comely woman with ample petticoats and a big white apron.

Naturally, there could be only the one theme of conversation. The tears ran down Mrs. Keen's ruddy cheeks as they talked. Susan was pale, more delicate-looking than ever, and her eyes, dry now, had a far-off look in them. How greatly she put Mrs. Carlyon in mind of Katherine that lady did not choose to say.

"I can understand all your distress, all your trouble," spoke she in a sympathising tone. "And the *uncertainty* as to what became of her must be harder to bear than all else."

"*Something* must have interrupted her when she had just begun to undress; that seems to be evident, ma'am," said the mother. "She had taken off her cap and apron, her collar and ribbon--and all else that she had on disappeared with her. The question is, what that something could be. Susan thinks--but I'm afraid she thinks a great deal that is but idleness," broke off the mother, with a fond pitying glance at the girl.

"What does Susan think?" asked Mrs. Carlyon.

Susan lifted her white face to answer. The vacant look it mostly wore was very perceptible now; her tone became dull and monotonous.

"Ma'am," she said, "I think that when Katherine had just got those few things off, somebody came to her door, and--and----"

"And what?" said Mrs. Carlyon, for the girl had stopped.

"I wish I knew what. I wish I could think what; but I can't. Some days I think he must have taken her out of the room, and some days I think he killed her in it. It fairly dazes me, ma'am."

"Whom do you mean by 'he'?" again questioned Mrs. Carlyon, wondering whether the girl had anyone in particular in her mind.

"It must have been some stranger, some wicked man that we don't know-- or a woman," answered Susan, slowly. "Miss Winter had gone down then, and was out of hearing."

"But there was no stranger at Heron Dyke that night, either man or woman," objected Mrs. Carlyon. "Only the women-servants, old Aaron, the Squire, and Miss Winter."

"Somebody might have been hid in the house. She'd not go out of the room, ma'am, of her own accord."

"Not unless she had something to go for," said Mrs. Carlyon; "though I do not see what it was likely to be," she slowly added. "Or, if she did go out, why did she not go back again?"

"Ma'am," spoke the landlady, "against that theory there's the fact that she left the candle behind her. Miss Winter found it burnt down to the socket. If she had gone out of the room she would have taken the light with her."

"It is a great mystery," mused Mrs. Carlyon. "What could have become of her? Where can she be?"

"She was hurt in some way, or else frightened," said Susan. "Screams of terror, those two were, that I heard."

"With regard to those screams," returned Mrs. Carlyon, "the singular thing is that no one else heard them; no one in the house."

"Tom Barnet heard them, ma'am, the coachman's boy," interposed the mother, smoothing down the sleeve of her lilac cotton gown. "I can't think there's any doubt but that the screams came from Katherine. I'd give--I'd give all I'm worth to know where she is, dead or alive."

"She is inside Heron Dyke!" cried Susan, her voice taking a sound of awe.

"Nonsense," somewhat impatiently rebuked Mrs. Carlyon. "You ought to know that it cannot be, Susan."

Susan lifted her patient face, a pleading kind of look on it.

"Ma'am, she's there; she's there. I've seen her at the window of her room in the moonlight; it's three times now."

"Run in, Susie; I thought I heard the gentleman's bell," spoke her mother, and Susan gathered up her work and went. But Mrs. Carlyon saw it was only a ruse to get rid of her.

"She is growing almost silly upon the point, ma'am," Mrs. Keen began; "thinking she sees her sister at the window. I believe it's all fancy, for my part; nothing but the reflection of some tree branches cast on the window-blind by the moon."

"Why don't you forbid her going up to Heron Dyke in the dark?" sensibly asked Mrs. Carlyon. "It cannot be good for her."

"Because, ma'am, I'm feared that if I did, her mind would quite lose its balance," replied the mother. "I do stop her all I can; but I dare not do it quite always. The going up there to watch the windows for Katherine has become like meat and drink to her."

Mrs. Carlyon sighed. Throughout the interview the landlady had never ceased to wipe her tears away; they rose in spite of her. It was altogether a very distressing case, and Mrs. Carlyon wished it had occurred anywhere rather than at Heron Dyke.

"I suppose Katherine had no trouble? She was not in bad spirits?" she remarked.

"She had no trouble in the world that I know of; there was none that she could have. Susan met her in Nullington the morning of the very day it happened, and she was as blithe as could be. Miss Winter was making some underthings for the poor little neglected Tysons, and found she had not got enough material to cut out the last, so she sent Katherine for another yard of it, charging her to make haste. Well, ma'am, Susan met her, as I tell you; and, as Katherine was going back to the Hall, she saw me standing at the door here. 'I hear you have heard from John, mother,' she called out; and her face was bright and her voice cheerful as a lark's; 'Susan says she will bring me up the letter this evening.' 'Come in for it now, child,' I answered her. 'No,' she said, 'if I came in I should be sure to stop talking with you, and Miss Winter is waiting for what I've been to fetch. You'll let Susan bring it up this evening, mother.' 'If the weather holds up,' I answered, glancing at the skies, which seemed to threaten a fall of some sort; 'but her cold hangs about her, and I can't let her go out at night if rain comes on.' With that she nodded to me and ran on laughing; she used to think it a joke, the care I took of Susan. No, ma'am," concluded the mother, "my poor Katherine was in no trouble of mind."

Mrs. Carlyon went back to the Hall full of thought. One thing she could not understand--how it was, if Katherine had screamed, that she should have been heard out of doors, and not indoors. And Mrs. Carlyon, that same evening, when she was dressing for dinner, sent Higson for Dorothy Stone, telling the maid she need not come back; and she put the question to Dorothy.

Mrs. Stone went into a twitter forthwith. The least allusion to the subject invariably sent her into one. No, the cry had not been heard indoors, she answered. Neither by the master nor Miss Ella, who were shut up in the oak sitting-room, nor by her and the maids in the kitchen. But the north wing was ever so far off, and she did not think they could have heard it. The only one about the house was Aaron, and he ought to have heard it, if any scream had been screamed.

"And he did not hear it?" spoke Mrs. Carlyon.

"Aaron heard nothing, ma'am," replied the housekeeper. "The corridors and passages, above and below, were just as silent as they always are, inside this great lonely house at night; and that's as silent as the grave. Aaron was locking up, and could well have heard any scream in the north wing. He was longer than usual that night, as it chanced, for he got his oil, and was oiling the front-door lock, which had grown a bit rusty. Had there been any noise in the north wing, screaming, or what not, he could not have failed to hear it: and for that reason he holds to it to this day that there was none; that the screams Susan Keen professed to hear were just her flighty fancy."

"And do you think so, Dorothy?"

"Ma'am, I don't know what to say," answered the old woman, pushing back her grey hair, as she was apt to do when in a puzzle of thought. "I should think it was the girl's fancy but for Tom Barnet. Tom holds to it that the two screams were there, sure enough, just as Susan does; the last a good deal fainter than the first."

"There's the dinner-gong!" exclaimed Mrs. Carlyon, as the sound boomed up from below. "And none of my ornaments on yet. Clasp this bracelet for me, will you, Dorothy. We will talk more of this another time. Dr. Jago dines here to-night, I hear: what a fancy the Squire seems to have taken to him!"

CHAPTER XII.

FAREWELL

The day of departure was here, bringing with it Ella's last afternoon at Heron Dyke for several weeks, or it might be, for several months to come. Her uncle's will in the matter, combined with Mrs. Carlyon's, had conquered her own. Dr. Jago added his influence in the shape of a warning, that his patient must on no account be irritated by contradiction or he would not be answerable for the consequences.

Ella felt that there was no other course open to her than to yield; but she cried many bitter tears in secret. She did not want to leave home at all just now, although ten days or a fortnight in Paris might have proved a pleasant change. But to go away for a whole winter, and so far away too, was certainly something that she had never contemplated. It was true that Mr. Denison seemed better in health, much better; but, for all that, she had a presentiment which she could not get rid of, that if she left him now she should never see him again in this world. Still, she had to obey her uncle's wishes.

And now the last afternoon was here, and waning quickly. She had bidden farewell to Maria Kettle, to Lady Cleeve, and all other friends; she had taken her last walk along the shore, her last look at the garden and grounds, each familiar spot had been visited in turn; and it seemed to her as though she were bidding them farewell for ever. She and Mrs. Carlyon were going up to London by the evening train; they would spend a couple of days in town and then cross by the Dover boat.

Through the leaden-paned windows of Mr. Denison's sitting-room the rays of the October sun shone wanly, lighting up a point of panelling here and there, or lending a momentary freshness, a forgotten grace, to one or other of the faded portraits on the walls. As the sick man sat there in his big leathern chair, his dim eyes wandered now and again to the motto of his family where, lighted by the sun, it shone out in colours blood-red and golden high up in the central window. There was a ring of worldly pride in the words, of the strength and the glory of possession. "What I have I hold." How much longer would he, the living head of the house, continue to hold anything of that which earth had given him? Already the cold airs of the grave blew about him: already he seemed to hear the dread words, "Ashes to ashes," while from the sexton's clay-stained fingers a little earth was crumbled on to his coffin lid. "What I have I hold." Vain mockery! when the grim Captain whispers in your ear, and bids you follow him.

Ella sat on a low hassock at her uncle's knee. One of her hands was tightly grasped in his, while his other hand stroked her hair fondly. It was a gaunt and bony hand, and seemed all unfitted for such loving usages. They spoke to each other in low tones, with frequent pauses between. To any stranger there, who could have heard their voices but not their words, it would have seemed as if they were discussing some trivial topic of every-day life. But both Ella and the Squire had determined that they would keep a strict guard over their feelings. Neither of them would let the other see the emotions at work below, though each might guess at their existence. Dr. Jago had warned the young lady to make her parting as quiet a one as possible: excitement of any kind was hurtful to his patient. Mr. Denison's proud hard nature could not entirely change itself, even at a time like the present; besides which, he wanted to make the separation as little distressing to Ella as might be. It maybe that he felt that if she were to break down at the last moment and betray much emotion, his own veneer of stoicism might not prove of much avail.

"I think, Uncle Gilbert, you understand clearly the arrangements made for our communicating with each other while I am away?" said Ella.

"I think so, my pretty one. You can go over them again if you like."

"I will write to you once a week, and send you a telegram as often as we leave one place for another. Hubert Stone will write to me in your name every Monday to save you from fatigue; and you must write sometimes yourself. Should your health change in the slightest degree for the worse, he will telegraph to me without a moment's delay."

"That's it: I shan't forget," said Mr. Denison. "What with this telegraphing, and one thing or another, it will seem as if you were no farther away than the next village."

"I shall feel that we are very far apart," said Ella. "You forget what a long time it takes to travel from Italy to Heron Dyke."

"Nothing like the time it used to take when I was a young spark. I remember when I went the grand tour as it was called--but there, there, we have something else to talk about now. Anyhow, railroads are a wonderful invention."

There were twenty things on Ella's tongue that she would have liked to speak of, but that it might be more wise to refrain from. Dr. Jago's warning words rarely left her thoughts.

"Be sure to wrap yourself up warmly when you go out in the carriage, uncle."

"Ay, ay, dearie, I won't forget."

"I shall come back to you the first week in the new year. Two months will be quite long enough to be away from home."

"We have agreed to see about that, you know, my lassie. I will send you word when I feel that I want you, and then you will come. Not before, I think--not before."

It was a topic that Ella dared not pursue further. She kissed his hand with tears in her eyes. He patted her cheek lovingly.

"Oh! why does he persist so strongly in sending me away?" she thought. "Hubert let fall a word--an inadvertent one, I think--the other night, that they feared I should be melancholy in this gloomy old house in the winter. It is gloomy now, but I could have put up with that very well."

"If I get on as famously for the next month or two as I have for the last three weeks," said the Squire, "I shall be able to drive to the station and meet you when you come home. And then when the sun comes out warm next spring, I can take your arm, and we can walk again in the peach alley as we used to do. Why not?"

Was there something wistful in his voice, as he spoke thus, that caused Ella to glance up quickly into his face.

"Are you sure, uncle, that you are really as much stronger and better as you say you are?" she asked quickly, and with ill-concealed anxiety.

One of his old suspicious flashes came into his eyes, but it died away next moment.

"Am I sure, dearie? Why--why, what makes you ask that? You can see for yourself that I'm better. Yes, Jago's making another man of me--another man."

"Tell me the truth, uncle," she exclaimed passionately, "*why* is it that you are driving me away? I am sure there is some special reason for it."

For a moment or two the Squire did not answer: his face was working with some inward excitement, his fingers, stroking the hand he held, trembled visibly.

"The house is getting uncanny, child," he said at last, "and I won't suffer my pretty one to be in it through the dark months. Before another winter comes round, perhaps the mystery will be solved; I hope it will be. Any way, we shall by that time have become more reconciled to it."

"But, uncle----"

"No objection, my dear one. You have never made any to my will yet, and you must not begin now. Understand, child: I am sending you away for *the best*; the best for you and for me; and you must be guided by me implicitly, as you ever have been."

Ella sighed--and would not let him see her tears.

The yellow sunlight faded and vanished from the gloomy room, the old portraits on the walls shrank farther back into the twilight of their frames and were lost to view, the log on the hearth crackled and glowed more redly bright as darkness crept on apace, and still those two sat hand in hand, speaking a few words now and then, but mostly silent. At length the moment of departure came, the carriage was at the door, and Mrs. Carlyon entered, ready for travelling.

The Squire grasped the back of his chair with one hand; he was trembling in every limb. Mrs. Carlyon bade him goodbye quietly and without fuss. He kissed her, and held her hand.

"Gertrude," he said, "into your hands I commit my one earthly treasure. I charge you with the care of it. Never forget!"

Ella clung to him, and laid her head upon his breast. His rugged features worked convulsively. He lifted her face tenderly between his hands and kissed her several times.

"Let me stay with you, uncle. Why drive me away?" she said imploringly.

For a moment there came into his eyes a gleam of agony terrible to see: it was a look which Ella never forgot.

"No--no--it must not be: I am doing for the best," he repeated, in a hoarse whisper; "I tell it you. Farewell, my sweetest and best--farewell. Go now--go now," he whispered, as he sank into his chair and pointed to the door.

Hubert Stone, looking every inch a gentleman, attended them to the station, sitting on the box with Barnet. Higson went inside with the ladies. At the station, Ella took Hubert aside for a private word.

"You will be sure not to forget your instructions, Hubert?"

"I shall not forget one of them, Miss Ella," was his answer. "You may rely upon that."

"You must watch my uncle narrowly. Should you see the approach of any change in him, telegraph to me. Question your friend, Dr. Jago, continually of his state. Say nothing to my uncle. I will take the responsibility if you send for me. You will always know where we are, for I shall keep you well informed."

The young man bowed. He was afraid to let his eyes meet hers: she might perhaps have fathomed the burning secret that lay half hidden there--his passionate love.

"I trust you, Hubert remember that: I have only you to trust to now at Heron Dyke. And now, goodbye."

Hubert clasped the hand she extended to him. And the next moment he assisted her into the carriage.

"Ah, if I might dare to think it would ever be!" he groaned, watching the train as it puffed out of the station. "And, I do think it may, I fear, more than is wholesome for me; for the hope is little short of madness."

At that time the county of Norfolk had been startled from its propriety by the ill-judged action of a young lady belonging to the family of one of its magnates. She had married one of her father's men-servants. Hubert Stone lit his cigar, and quitted the station to return home, thinking of this. Strange to say, he saw in it some encouragement for himself.

"If Miss G. can stoop to marry a low fellow like that, surely there's nothing so very outrageous in my aspiring to Ella Winter! I am well educated; I can behave as a gentleman; I am good-looking. There's nothing against me but birth--and fortune. She will have enough of the latter if she comes into Heron Dyke--and if Jago's clever, I expect she will. Any way her fortune will be a fair one, for the Squire must have saved hoards of money. She can well afford to dispense with money in whomsoever she may marry: and if she can only be brought to overlook the disadvantage of my birth----"

"Good-evening, Mr. Stone. And how's the Squire?"

Hubert's dreams were thus cut short. He answered the question mechanically, and stopped to talk to the chance acquaintance who had accosted him.

Meanwhile Ella and Mrs. Carlyon were speeding London-ward as fast as the Great Eastern Railway could carry them. At Cambridge there was a stoppage for two or three minutes. Suddenly Mrs. Carlyon uttered an exclamation of surprise.

"Ella, look! Look there! that is surely Mr. Conroy. He is looking for a seat."

Ella bent forward. The next moment Mr. Conroy recognised them. He advanced to the carriage window, and raised his hat.

"Who, in the name of wonder, expected to see you here?" exclaimed Mrs. Carlyon, as she held out her hand. "I thought you were in Ashantee."

"It is one of my privileges to turn up in unexpected places," he answered. Then he shook hands with Ella and inquired after Mr. Denison.

"Were you looking for a place?--are you going to town?" asked Mrs. Carlyon. "If you don't mind travelling with unprotected females, there's plenty of room here."

And, thanking her, into the carriage stepped Edward Conroy, with the frank look and smile that Ella remembered so well.

"Well, if he is not a cool one!" thought the discerning Higson to herself. "I'd not mind answering for it that in some way he got to know Miss Ella would be here, and came down from town on purpose to meet her. I can read it in his eyes. There's no answering for what these venturesome young gents will do!"

"And will you kindly explain to us, Mr. Conroy, what business you have to be in England when you ought to be sketching black people out in Africa?"

"Within twenty-four hours of the time I was to have sailed, I received a telegram informing me that my father was dangerously ill. Under the circumstances, I could not sail; I had to go to him instead. I stayed some time with him, left him better, and then found that Dempster had been sent in my place."

"And a very fortunate thing too."

Conroy laughed.

"You lack enterprise, Mrs. Carlyon. I am afraid that you would never do for a special correspondent. Do you expect to make a long stay in London this time?" he asked, turning to Ella.

"We intend starting for the Continent the day after tomorrow," answered Mrs. Carlyon. "You had better come and dine with us tomorrow evening: there will be no one but ourselves and Mr. Bootle."

"I shall be very happy to do so," replied Conroy. "What place are you going to make your head-quarters while you are away?"

"I had some thoughts of San Remo, but we shall probably be birds of passage and not stay long in any one place."

Conroy saw that Ella was silent, and guessed the parting with her uncle had been a sad one. What he did not know was, how sweet his presence and company were to her. She had been thinking of him that very day--thinking of him sadly as of one whom she might never see again; and now he was here, sitting opposite to her. What rare chance had brought him?--She did not talk much, she was satisfied to hear his voice and see his face; at present she craved nothing more. The journey she so much dreaded had all at once been invested with a charm, with an unexpected sweetness, which she never tried to analyse: enough for her that it was there.

Conroy saw the ladies into their carriage at the London terminus, and bade them goodbye till the following evening. Then he lighted a cigar and set out to walk to his rooms in the Adelphi. He was in a musing mood, debating some question with himself as he walked along.

"Shall I tell Mrs. Carlyon a certain secret, or shall I not?" he thought. "Would she keep it to herself? No, no; better be on the safe side," he presently decided: "and the time is hardly ripe to tell it to anyone. What would Squire Denison say if it were whispered to him?"

On this very evening, while these ladies were on their way to London, a strange thing happened at Heron Dyke.

It was about eight o'clock. Fitch the saddler had come up from Nullington about some little matter of business, and Aaron Frost sent one of the housemaids to fetch him a certain whip that was hanging up in the hall. As Martha left the room with her candle she met her fellow-servant, Ann, and the latter turned to accompany her. The girls never cared to go about the big house singly after dark. They went along chattering merrily, and thinking of anything rather than unpleasant subjects. Martha was repeating a ludicrous story just told in the kitchen by the saddler, and could hardly tell it for laughing.

As in many old mansions, round three sides of the entrance-hall there ran an oaken gallery, some twenty feet above the ground, from which various doors gave access to different parts of the house. This gallery was reached from the hall by a broad and shallow flight of stairs.

"How cold this place always strikes one," exclaimed Ann, as they entered the hall.

"It would want many a dozen of candles to light it up properly," remarked Martha.

Having found the whip, they turned to retrace their steps, when Martha, happening to glance up at the gallery, gave utterance to a low cry, and grasped her companion by the arm. Ann's eyes involuntarily followed the same direction, and a similar cry of intense terror burst from her lips.

They saw the face of the missing girl--the face of Katherine Keen, gazing down upon them from the gallery. The face was very pale; white as that of the dead. The figure was leaning over the balustrade of the gallery, and its eyes gazed down into theirs with a sad, fixed, weary look. It seemed to be clothed in something dark, pulled partly over its head and grasped at the throat by the white, slender fingers. For fully half a minute, the two girls stood and stared up at the figure in sheer incapability, and the figure looked sadly down upon them. At length it moved--it turned--it took a step forward, and the servants, both of them, distinctly heard the sound of a faint far-away sigh. Could it be possible that the figure meant to come downstairs? The spell that had held the girls was broken; with low smothered cries of terror they turned and fled, clinging to each other.

How the one dropped the whip and the other the candle, and how they at length gained the kitchen, and burst into it with their terror-stricken faces and their unhappy tale, they never knew. Fitch the saddler gazed in open-eyed amazement, as well he might; the deaf and stolid cook looked in from the cooking-kitchen--in which congenial place she preferred to sit, surrounded by her saucepans.

The girls sobbed forth all the dismal story. Their mistress, Mrs. Stone, flung her apron over her head as she listened, and sank back in her chair in dismay equal to theirs. But old Aaron was so indignant, so scandalised, at what he called their senseless folly, that he lost his breath in a rage, and gave each of them a month's warning on the spot.

END OF VOL. I.

Milton Keynes UK
Ingram Content Group UK Ltd.
UKHW012313040624
443649UK00007B/608